Mystery at Mappins

Mystery

at Mappins

By Irene Byers

ILLUSTRATED BY VICTOR AMBRUS

CHARLES SCRIBNER'S SONS   NEW YORK

42764

Contents

1 . . . *Surprise from Father*

IAN MEREDITH pushed aside the thin muslin curtain, rubbed away the film that his breath had made on the window, and peered out along the length of Somerville Avenue. Behind him, shorter by one foot and younger by four years, his brother Paul hopped impatiently from one foot to another.

"Stop pushing," said Ian.

Paul prodded him in the back.

"I wouldn't have to, if you didn't hog all the window space."

From where she lay full length on the homemade rug, tickling the battle-scarred ear of their cat, Mr. Smithers, Leonie said, "Penny for the fine box, even if Mother isn't here to hear you using that word."

"I don't care." Paul was in a mutinous frame of mind. "He is a hog. He's the hoggiest hog I've ever met. If he hadn't switched the set on and off so quickly the valve wouldn't have gone."

Paul felt that his accusation was justified, and wished for the first time that there were not alternative programs on television. That was the worst of having an older brother, he told himself. Ian always had his own way and now, all because he had mistreated the set, Paul could not follow the sixth and final episode in the serial and watch his beloved cowboy hero shoot from the hip, scale rock-strewn hillsides on his magnificent white charger and bring in the gang strung out like a bunch of bananas at the end of his rope.

Leonie yawned and glanced at the clock on the mantel-piece.

"In any case you're both being very silly," she remarked. "You know Daddy never gets home a minute before six o'clock. And even if he were five minutes earlier it wouldn't make any difference. It isn't a valve that's burned out. It's the tube that's gone."

"Oh, do shut up, Lee," said Ian, feeling as frustrated as his younger brother. "Girls don't know anything about such things. But just suppose you're right for once. Isn't that all the more reason why we should catch Dad before he gets into the house? Old Mr. Porter doesn't close his shop until half past six, and he might be sporting enough to lend us a set while ours is being repaired."

Leonie did not answer, and a moment later Paul, who had nuzzled under his brother's arm to a frontal position, suddenly gave a shout.

8

"There's Dad now, passing the mailbox. Bother! He's stopped to talk to Mr. Phillips." He mimicked their neighbor's dry, somewhat pedantic manner of speaking. "And how do you find business, Mr. Meredith? Taking the rough with the smooth, I suppose. Ah, well, while we have a loaf of bread in the larder and a pint of milk on the doorstep, we mustn't grumble."

Ian laughed and so did his sister, the imitation was so exact. Mr. Phillips was a kindly soul, who frequently held out the bait of two shillings if one of them would cut the rank-smelling privet hedge bordering his narrow front garden. Platitudes, however, poured from his lips like beans from an unstoppered jar.

All at once Leonie felt ashamed of herself for laughing. Mr. Phillips could not help being dull and a bit of a bore.

"I'd die," she thought, "if I had to live his life—catch the eight-thirty train every morning, work in a dusty office among equally dusty ledgers and return every night to a shabby, dull home. That's what I'd do. I'd die."

The pattern of her thoughts made her sit up with a jerk. She might be thinking of Mr. Phillips, but the description fitted her own father's way of life exactly. There was not much excitement in his life either, except for his main holiday in August; then frequently it rained, or the boarding house gave poor value for money hardly saved.

Her glance fell on the pipe rack fitted to the wall beside the fireplace. That represented his final act of self-denial, for in order to buy the television set her father had been forced to give up smoking. True, he had not seemed to mind all that much. Where his family's interests were concerned,

9

his self-discipline was of the cast-iron variety. But theirs was not, Leonie told herself. They fought, squabbled and bickered, especially the boys. And she herself was not without blame.

With a feeling of remorse she rose to her feet, and pushing aside her brothers, looked out of the window. Her father was no longer talking to Mr. Phillips, but walking with a slow, measured tread, as if postponing the moment of opening his own front gate. A moment later the latch clicked and both boys made for the dining-room door. Their sister turned swiftly.

"Ian, don't," she pleaded. "Daddy looks so tired. At least let him have his supper first."

"Won't be any good," he answered. "He's bound to ask why we haven't got the set on. We always have when he comes home."

Paul counted on his fingers.

"Monday . . . Tuesday . . . Wednesday. Oh, goody. It's Thursday and sausages."

Leonie's hand flew to her mouth.

"Heavens, I've forgotten! It's Mummy's day at the clinic. They ought to have been sizzling ages ago."

She hurried along the dark, narrow hall to the kitchen, hearing as she did so Paul's final admonition to stab the villains well to prevent them from bursting.

Ian, meantime, had reached the front door. Opening it, he stood with legs astride, watching his father look at the sky, where starlings, their purple, mottled wings outstretched, wheeled eastwards toward the city. Even to a casual observer, the likeness between the two was striking. Both had coarse,

10

rather springy, brown hair sweeping back from broad fore-
heads. Both had brown eyes, prominent noses and squarely
cut chins. The difference lay in the flesh. Ian's cheeks were
rounded and pink, and his mouth was inclined to droop at
the slightest provocation. His father's flesh was drawn tightly
about the jaws, and his mouth, schooled by years of patience,
was narrow-lipped and gently curving.

Patience also lay in the set of his shoulders as, turning,
he saluted his sons. Ian knew a moment of compunction.
Leonie was right. His father did look tired. Before he could
restrain his brother, however, Paul burst out, "Dad. Something terrible's happened. The television set's broken."

"Good."

With an arm around each boy, Mr. Meredith propelled
Paul and Ian into the hall. Separated by the width of his
body, they looked at each other in dismay.

"What did you say, Dad?" Paul was convinced that
he could not have heard right.

His father hung his shabby hat on a peg.

"I said, good. It's the best bit of news I've heard for
many a long day."

"You don't mean it. You're joking, Dad." Ian's tone
was anxious.

His father stooped to stroke the arched back of the cat
as it rubbed against his legs. Then he smiled upwards.

"On the contrary, I was never more serious. Oh, hello,
Lee. Your mother not back from the clinic yet?"

Leonie shook her head, and pushing her father into his
own armchair, shut the door against the drifting smell of
hot fat. Then, perched on the arm, she tweaked a strand of

11

his thinning hair into a point. As a hat will when worn at an unaccustomed angle, it gave him a clownish look.

"Don't do that, Lee," he protested, brushing the strands flat. "At the moment I need to look my most impressive."

"Which means they've told you. I warned them to let you have your supper first."

"Diplomacy wouldn't have made any difference. I've no intention of having the set mended, not for a while, at any rate."

There was a moment of shocked silence. At length, Leonie said, "Don't you like television?"

"Very much, if it encourages people to think and act more adventurously. But that hasn't happened in your case. No, Ian, let me finish. I don't want to make heavy weather of this, but slowly and surely you're becoming a trio of . . . of goggle-eyed morons."

Paul glanced uncertainly at his father.

"What's a moron? I thought it was a terribly expensive kind of sweet."

Leonie laughed delightedly.

"That's a marron glacé, you idiot. A moron is . . ." She looked helplessly at her father. "I . . . I expect we deserve the term, but what is it exactly?"

Mr. Meredith reached for a dictionary standing on a shelf of the low alcove bookcase. Running his finger down the appropriate column, he read out: " 'A somewhat feeble-minded person; one who remains throughout life at the mental age of eight.' "

Ian's cheeks flushed with anger.

"Then I think that's a mean and beastly description of

us. You can't call me half-witted because I like watching the Test Matches. It was the last half-hour of play I was after this evening."

"No, but when did you last play yourself?" Mr. Meredith put the dictionary back.

Ian stared at the floor and scuffed the corner of the rug up with his foot.

"You can't play cricket properly in a playground with chalk marks on the wall for stumps."

"But you could play, that's the point," amended his father. "Cricket apart, what happened to that workbox on legs you started making for your mother?"

"It's still minus the lid and legs," answered Leonie.

To relieve his own sense of embarrassment, Ian turned on her.

"You needn't look so smug. Who begged so hard for a set of oils last Christmas, so that she could start filling the house with her miserable little daubs? The only masterpiece you ever finished is blocking up the window Paul smashed in the green house when he was playing at being a thug and shooting off his horrible little popgun."

"It isn't a popgun," contradicted Paul indignantly. "It's a five-barreled repeater, and you're not to call me a thug."

"Well, whatever you are, you're a beastly young bore. Honestly, Dad. He's the end. Why, a chap can't even go into the bathroom to clean his teeth without having a rope swish around his head from behind."

"I've got to practice lassoing sometimes and on someone," his brother retorted, "and you're an awfully good target because you spend such a long time looking at yourself in the mirror. I can't think why. You must know what you look like by now."

"It's all wrapped up with pimples and wishful thinking," his sister suggested naughtily. "Ian's longing for the day when he can use Dad's razor." With a gesture that infuriated him, she ran a finger over his chin. "What a shame. Not even so much as one tiny bristle."

Ian pushed her away, and as she cannoned into Paul, he in turn trod on the cat's tail. Mr. Smithers, well versed in the art of self-defense, yowled, shot out a paw and left retaliatory weals below the offender's knee. In the hubbub that ensued, all three turned reproachful eyes on their father, who was laughing.

"Oh dear! Oh dear! And to think that all this started because a knob failed to work."

Paul looked down at his injured leg.

"I don't think it's funny. I shall probably get blood poisoning and run a temperature for days and days."

"You probably will if you rub the wound with that grubby hand," remarked his father. "Run and get the disinfectant, Lee, and bring a roll of bandage."

As she hurried to obey, her mother entered the room. Short, plump and placid, and wearing her suit and the close-fitting hat that brought out the fairness of her hair and heightened the blue of her eyes, she gazed from one to the other in perplexity.

"Now what was all that commotion about? And what have you done to Mr. Smithers that he didn't stop to greet me?"

"What has he done to me, you mean," said Paul, thrust-

14

ing out his knee in the hope that his mother, at least, would prove sympathetic. He was disappointed.

"Good gracious me! It's only a scratch, and knowing Smithers, I feel sure he had just cause to be provoked. But even if you were having one of your family squabbles, it's a nice change not to have that thing blaring away in the corner."

"Actually, that's what started it," said Ian. "It's broken, and Dad says he won't have it fixed, and he's been lighting into us ever since."

"Only in the intervals." His father's eyes twinkled. "I've been trying to awaken the spirit of initiative, Ellen."

"Good for you, John." Mrs. Meredith removed her hat. "Goodness knows, it's time we had a little of that commodity around the house."

"Oh, don't you start on us, too," said Ian. He paused and looked at his father. "Do you mind if I say something personal, Dad?"

"Not in the very least, Ian. Go ahead."

"I don't know how to put it. It's all very well to talk about initiative or adventure or whatever you like to call it, but you can't say your own life is very exciting."

"Ian! I will not have you speak to your father like that. You ought to be ashamed when you know how hard he works for us." For once his mother was shocked into something like anger.

"It's all right, my dear. Go on, Ian."

Feeling more and more uncomfortable under his mother's direct gaze and the withering look Leonie gave him as she handed the tape to their father, he went on: "I . . . I . . .

15

don't mean to be rude, Dad. But you must admit that being an insurance agent is a pretty routine sort of existence. Oh, I know you go to your club two evenings a week."

"That's where you're wrong, my lad." Mr. Meredith poured a little disinfectant onto some cotton wool and ignored his younger son's gasp as he applied it. "I haven't been near my club for years. I've been attending evening classes."

"Evening classes!" exclaimed his wife. "Are you serious, John? How could you keep a secret like that from me? I've never seen you read anything but a novel in the evening."

"Dust jackets can be deceptive, my dear." Her husband took a book from the shelf, and opening it at random, read out a couple of sentences on the irrigation of dry, infertile land.

For the first time in her married life, Mrs. Meredith felt shut out, and she found it difficult to keep the reproach from her voice when she said, "We've shared most things together. Why didn't you tell me about this?"

"Because I might have failed. As it is, you see before you a theoretically qualified estate manager."

Leonie flung her arms around his neck and placed her cool cheek against his flushed one.

"Daddy! How wonderful! It's the most surprising news ever to burst upon the family." As her mother sank heavily into a chair, she added, "Don't you think so, Mummy?"

"Before I say anything, I'd like to know what made your father decide upon such a step."

As he had so often done in past moments of stress, Mr. Meredith reached towards his pipe rack, then let his hand fall in a gesture of resignation.

16

"Call it a hangover from boyhood days if you like. I never wanted to become an insurance agent. But when I left school the need to get a job was urgent; then, while I was still dreaming of open spaces and the feel of the wind in my face, fate in the shape of a slip of a girl with fair hair and blue eyes decided me."

"If only you'd told me, John. I'd have waited years, if necessary."

"Couldn't take the risk," her husband replied, laughing. "You were too much of a beauty. Do you know, children, every boy for miles around came knocking at her front door."

"Wish she'd given a little bit to me," said Leonie. "Good looks, I mean. They're so much more comfortable than beauty. It's horribly dull being plain."

"Rubbish!" cried her mother. "You're both talking nonsense. When you've filled out a bit, you'll do very nicely, because you've got . . . "

"I know. I've got good bone structure. Aunt Jane's always telling me that, but I wish she wouldn't. She makes me sound as if I were a horse being judged on points."

"A filly, you mean," chortled Paul, his good spirits fully recovered. "Lee's a filly! Lee's a filly!"

"That's quite enough, Paul," said his mother. "The question is, what happens now?"

"That's what I'd like to know," broke in Ian. Lacking the imagination of his sister, he could only see in his father's confession a gesture that led nowhere. "If all you do with a diploma is to frame it, you aren't any better off than when you started, are you?"

His father's look was almost one of pity.

"Then you haven't understood a word of what I've been

17

trying to say to you." He ran a finger over the smooth, pink palm of his daughter's hand. Like her cheek it was cool and as soft and as pliant as one of the ferns he tried to grow in his small greenhouse. "But Lee has," he added.

She imprisoned his finger and squeezed it, her face wearing what Ian always thought of as her Vista-Vision expression.

"I think I have," she said slowly. "I think Daddy means that striving after something and proving to yourself that you can reach or do it is what matters."

"Exactly." Her father's foot tucked the corner of the rug flat. "Traveling hopefully is the phrase someone once used. Well, I've traveled, and I've had a lot of fun in the arriving." He rose. "Now let us also travel hopefully to the kitchen."

"The sausages!" gasped Leonie. "I'd forgotten all about them."

She ran from the room, and returned a moment later carrying the frying pan with the charred remains of their supper.

"Mummy, I'm so sorry."

"Being sorry won't fill our tummies." Paul was distressed. He always looked forward to his weekly sausage supper. There was an endless variety of things you could do with the accompanying mashed potato—build stockades against marauding Indians, dam the thick, sluggish river of brown gravy and haul the brown sausage cannons into defensive positions along the ramparts. He felt cheated. "Honestly, Lee. You are a drip. You never do anything properly."

"No reproaches." His father brought out a handful of loose silver. "If anyone's to blame, I am. So by way of compensation, we'll feast off fish and chips."

18

"Goody!" shouted Paul, amply rewarded. "Next to sausages, I adore fish and chips. But mind old Bellamy gives you plenty of chips," he added warningly. "He can be awfully stingy at times. And don't let him palm off any rock salmon on you. Perhaps I'd better come with you, Lee. Batter is very deceiving."

Leonie pushed him back.

"No, thank you. The last time you came shopping with me, you insisted on tasting almost every cheese there was in the shop, and you put the greengrocer's back up by pinching his tomatoes until they burst. I'd rather go alone."

Nevertheless, she did not demur when Ian fell into step beside her. The evening was fine and clear, with the late July sun only now sinking below the line of chimney pots. Overhead, their stomachs filled with suburban bread, the starlings wheeled and circled before seeking their nightly roosting places. Yet neither brother nor sister had ears for their noisy chattering.

"It's been a surprising evening, hasn't it?" said Ian, as they turned into the busy main road. "To think that Dad could be so crafty." There was admiration in his voice. "He's made me feel pretty wormish. I don't know about estate management, but I bet the exams were jolly tough."

Leonie nodded. That their father should have hated his work so much was bad enough, but that his striving after something different should end in a parchment diploma was almost more than she could bear.

"If only he could change his job," she murmured. "Wouldn't it be wonderful?"

Ian did not reply, and striding ahead of her, entered the fish bar. Customers milled around the counter in a fog of pungent smoke. Not a few were dipping greasy fingers into newspaper cones and eating where they stood. Ian and Leonie edged their way closer to the vinegar-stained counter. Mr. Bellamy, who knew them well and had a liking for Lee, greeted her with a smile.

"Evening, my dear. What's your fancy this time? Same

20

as usual, or would you like to try a poor man's substitute for salmon? Comes off the bone sweet and clean."

"Skate, please," Leonie said firmly, "and lots of chips. Paul's starving."

"Lots it is then," he replied, moving toward the giant fryers and seizing a metal scoop. "Do me a favor, will you, and tear up some sheets of paper."

Leonie looked around for the customary pile of newspapers, but could see nothing but film and country magazines. Choosing one from the top of the pile, she began ripping the sheets apart. One fluttered to the floor and as she picked it up, her gaze was caught and held by four lines of print. For a moment she was lost to her surroundings, then a nudge from Ian and the thrusting of a large parcel under her nose recalled her. Hastily stuffing the sheet into her pocket, she handed over three half-crowns.

"Six-and-six from seven-and-six leaves one shilling change exactly." Mr. Bellamy rang up his machine. "There you are, my dear. Bellamy's the place when you're hungry, eh?"

Leonie smiled, and with the warmth of the parcel creeping into her fingers, followed her brother from the shop. Outside he looked at her curiously.

"What was so interesting about that piece of paper I saw you put in your pocket?"

"I'll tell you in three or four days from now," she replied. "Until then, it's my secret."

2 . . . *The Mysterious Telegram*

THAT NIGHT, long after the rest of the family were asleep, Leonie still tossed restlessly from one side of her bed to the other. She had counted sheep, read two chapters from her library book, but all to no avail. She was more wide awake than ever.

For the third time she switched on the bedside lamp and stared down at the sheet she had torn from the magazine. The four lines outlined in ink tantalized her with their promised opportunity. At length, she got out of bed, put on her woolen dressing gown and well-worn slippers and sat down at the small secondhand desk, which her Aunt Jane had so generously given her last Christmas. In it she kept the treasured hoardings of years—old letters, old theater programs, holiday snapshots and, most important of all, her red leather-bound journal. Opening it, she began filling in the entry for the day.

"It is nearly midnight," she wrote, "but because of what happened this evening I can't sleep. After living with Daddy for thirteen years I've suddenly discovered I don't know him at all. It was as if I'd set out to buy potatoes, and found instead that my shopping basket was full of strawberries. At least, that's how Daddy made me feel tonight. To think that he's been studying all this time without even telling Mummy. I couldn't have kept such a secret. He simply mustn't be allowed to let it all go to waste. And I'm going to see he doesn't although I've a horrid feeling that everyone else will think I'm interfering."

Interrupted by a sudden mewing, Leonie opened her bedroom door and scooped up Mr. Smithers.

"Can't you sleep either, you old night prowler?" she whispered. "No, you can't curl up in the down puff, but you can have my lap."

When Mr. Smithers had settled himself comfortably, she pushed her journal aside and reached for a sheet of note-paper. With her home address, the date and the words *Dear Sir* written down, she again paused. If it was easy to write in a journal, it ought to be easier to write to a complete stranger. But it wasn't. She fixed her gaze on a fly crawling upwards over the rose-sprigged wallpaper.

"When it reaches the ceiling, I'll begin," she told herself. The fly, however, paused, stretched its delicate transparent wings, then flew away to circle the light. "Very well," she further admonished herself, "I'll begin when Mr. Smithers stops purring." If anything the feline song became louder, and because she knew she was being foolish, she delayed no longer.

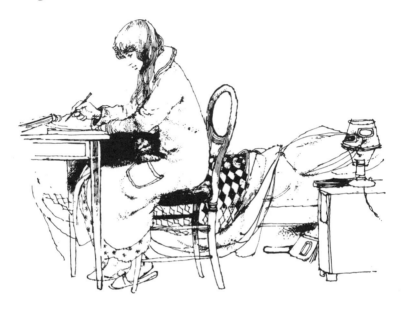

A quarter of an hour later the letter was sealed, addressed and stamped. Well aware that her resolution might weaken in the cold light of morning, and fearing the questions of her brothers, she put the cat on the floor, exchanged her dressing gown for a sweater and a light coat and crept down the stairs. Mr. Smithers followed. The well-oiled bolt on the front door slid back with scarcely a sound. Pulling the door to, but not shutting it, and with the cat now a mere black streak ahead of her, she went to mail the fateful letter.

Afterwards she was almost tempted to continue her

walk. The night was fine and the sky one vast, jeweled expanse. But at the sound of approaching footsteps she resisted the impulse. Leaving the night to the policeman and her cat, she returned to the chilly embrace of her own bed.

Next morning she failed to hear the rap on her door, and only awoke to the touch of her father's hand.

"Now then, Lazybones. This won't do. You don't want to blot your record by being late on the last day of the term. Mother's already called out that breakfast is ready."

Leonie sat up and rubbed her eyes. Mr. Smithers jumped onto the bed and rolled ecstatically on the down puff.

"Oh no, you don't," said Mr. Meredith. "Comforters are strictly taboo, you old sinner." Green eyes stared into brown as claws continued to leave pin pricks in the blue taffeta. "And there's another thing. How came you to be yowling on the back step at six o'clock this morning when the last time I had seen you you were lying on the dining-room rug?"

"We can tell you, Dad," said Paul, struggling to gain possession of the leather-bound book his brother held. "Lee must have let him out. She sat up late last night writing her journal. We found it on her desk when we came in much earlier." He grinned at Ian. "Read Dad the mushy bit about potatoes and strawberries."

Ian flicked over the pages.

"Here it is. Listen to this, Dad. It's priceless."

Horrified at the threatened exposure of her innermost thoughts and of her resolution to help, Leonie was speechless. She need not have worried. Before Ian could read so much as a word, her father held out his hand.

"Give me the journal at once, Ian." His voice sounded angry. "Haven't either of you boys yet learned that to pry into other people's secrets is just about the lowest form of meanness?"

Ian surrendered the book. "I don't see why. If it's so secret, why did she leave it lying about? All right. I'm sorry. We were only kidding. All the same, Lee has been up to something. There's guilt written all over her face."

Mr. Meredith glanced at his daughter. Her expression was both secretive and relieved. Not wishing to pry, he thrust the book into her hands, gave her shoulder a reassuring pat and bundled both his boys from the room.

Leonie locked away her journal, dressed quickly and came down to breakfast to find her brothers devising peace offerings. Paul poured the cream off the top of the milk onto her porridge. Ian, in his turn, forbore to leave her the burnt pieces of toast. Yet in spite of these overtures she remained aloof and refused to walk between them when they set out for school.

Ian had spoken more truly than he knew. She did feel guilty, and the sight of the mailbox, challenging in its scarlet, seemed to emphasize the enormity of her overnight folly. Two thoughts alone gave her comfort. The magazine from which she had torn the sheet was already three weeks old. Therefore, she argued, it was unlikely that she would get a reply. If she did, there was always the possibility of getting to the hall door first and hiding the letter.

The last day of the term was eventful. She enjoyed the final netball match, the returning of her books to the school library, the last-minute tidying up of her desk and the farewell

26

assembly in the hall. Five weeks of vacation lay ahead; if there was to be no fortnight by the sea this year, but a visit to Aunt Jane, who was resident matron at a school in Kent, they could still have fun. Aunt Jane might be a stickler for clean hands and tidy hair, and a "don't forget to wipe your feet on the mat" sort of person, but the grounds surrounding the expensive school offered unlimited games of tennis and cro- quet and swimming in the pool.

However, when she returned hungry for a tea of poached eggs and homemade fruit cake, disappointment awaited her. By the afternoon's mail a letter had come from Aunt Jane to say that an epidemic of measles had broken out in the last week of the term, and that the infirmary was full of sufferers forced to stay on for a fortnight's nursing.

"I can't see why that should stop us," grumbled Paul. "I've had measles and so has Ian."

"But your sister hasn't, though how she escaped I can't imagine," said his mother. "She took a daily interest in your spots, and got you to breathe over her at least four times an hour. No, we must just make the best of things. A vacation at home needn't be a punishment."

Paul put his hands over his ears.

"It will be for me, 'cause I know what you're going to say. There's always the National Gallery and the Natural His- tory Museum. I don't like pictures, and I hate stuffed animals in glass cases. Besides, no one ought to be asked to learn any- thing in the holidays."

Ian chuckled.

"Remember the last time we took him to the N.H.M.? I'll never forget the look on the museum attendant's face when he caught him trying to climb up the back legs of a prehistoric monster. He was ossified with horror himself.''

Everyone laughed at the recollection, and the gloom which had threatened to mar closing day lifted. Next morning, with breakfast over, Mr. Meredith accompanied his daughter shopping. Unlike most men, he enjoyed the bustle and noise of the nearby market, as did Leonie, although there were times when she wished they could buy from the more expensive stores without thought of saving pennies. Weighing the price of cauliflowers against the relative cheapness of greens, they at length came to the last item on the list, and with the basket filled, they returned home.

Mrs. Meredith met them in the hall.

"Oh, John, I am so glad you came straight home," she began. "A telegram's come for you. I opened it because I thought it might be urgent, but I don't understand it at all. It's signed Brett Clevedon. Is he a client of yours?"

Leonie's heart seemed to leap into her throat, and there was a cold, sick feeling in the pit of her stomach.

"Never heard of him," replied her husband cheerfully. "What does the message say?"

"Read for yourself," said his wife, handing him the telegram from the dining room mantelpiece.

" 'Letter received. Recommend you come to Mapledon by twelve-fifteen train for interview today.' Most mysterious." Mr. Meredith was plainly puzzled. "Could be that someone's bungled things at the office. Perhaps I'd better phone and find out. Old Brown will be there."

"You needn't do that," said Leonie. "I can explain. You see, Daddy, it was I who sent the letter."

28

"You!"

"Yes. Promise you won't be angry. I couldn't bear the thought of you just framing your diploma and doing nothing else about it. And you did say it was time we used our initiative."

Her father glanced helplessly from one to the other.

"Does anyone know what she's getting at?"

"I do, or at least I think I do," answered Ian, who with his brother had been listening quietly in the background. "It started in the fish shop when Lee was asked to tear up some magazines for wrapping. She put a sheet in her pocket and was awfully cagey about it. I bet you anything you like, she answered an advertisement."

"Did you, Lee?" asked her father.

"Yes. It invited applications from a married couple— the wife to help run the house, and the husband to act as manager of the property. The place is called Mappins. The advertisement didn't say anything about children, but I risked that."

"So that was your secret, and that's why you were burning the midnight oil," said Ian.

Leonie continued: "I didn't mean the explanation to come like this, and I've been hoping against hope that there wouldn't be a reply. But now the telegram's come, I'm glad. Please say you'll go, Daddy. This Mr. Clevedon must need a manager very badly if he's sent a telegram."

Her father looked bewildered.

"Maybe he does, but you're crazy, Lee, if you think I'd suit him. I'm only an estate agent on paper, but even if I had had any experience, the idea would still be preposterous. I couldn't possibly throw a secure job to the four winds just like that."

"I should jolly well think not," said Ian. "It's a relief to hear you say it, all the same."

"You keep out of this, my boy," snapped back his father. "It's not your opinion 1 want to hear, but your mother's."

"Oh, I think as you do, dear," she said quickly, giving him a sideways glance. "Naturally, the . . . the . . . very idea of you and me being able to suit this . . . Mr. Clevedon is absolutely ridiculous." Her husband flexed his muscles and rocked on his heels.

"I wouldn't put it as strongly as that. He'd have to go a long way before he'd find a better cook than you."

"Hear! Hear!" shouted Paul, making his contribution.

"As for me," continued his father, "I'm strong, and I'm not afraid of hard work. What's more, I'm not so old that I can't bring a few imaginative ideas into play, even if they do spring from textbook knowledge." He stared around as if daring any of them to contradict. "That's why so many of these smaller estates don't pay. They're still being run on feudal lines."

"I'm quite sure you're right," his wife said loyally. "Now supposing, only supposing, mind, that you did go for this interview. It wouldn't commit you to anything, would it?"

"That's true."

Feeling that his father needed only a little more persuasion to give in, Paul went into the attack.

"And it is a lovely day, and we *are* on vacation, so why don't we make the interview an excuse for having a picnic in the country?"

30

Without waiting to see the effect of his words, he ran to the sideboard where his keyless money box was kept and emptied the contents on to the table. Mixed up with the half-crowns, the shillings and the pence were a stick of chewing gum, a box of caps for his pistol and a half-dozen brightly colored cereal coupons.

"A veritable magpie's hoard," commented his father. "All right, Paul. You shall have your wish. A picnic it shall be, but since the outing is none of my arranging, you can each make a contribution of five shillings toward the fare."

The money was handed over, and immediately the family began preparations. Mr. Smithers was surrendered to the care of their next-door neighbor. Mrs. Meredith cut mounds of sandwiches, added a substantial cake and a bag of apples, and filled two thermos flasks with tea.

Leonie changed into a printed cotton dress, brushed and tied her hair back into a pony tail and took a cardigan for warmth. Ian offered his father the loan of his brightest tie, and when it was refused he wore it himself, with a royal-blue pullover.

Paul, who was almost beside himself with excitement, got in everybody's way, and when banished to the bathroom to wash, reappeared wearing a cowboy's hat, checked shirt, fringed leather leggings and a leather belt fitted with a gun holster.

Ian surveyed him with disgust.

"If you think I'm going to walk down the street with you in that outfit, you half-pint ruffian, you've got another think coming."

"Oh, let him alone," remonstrated his mother mildly, as she came out of the kitchen with her arms loaded. "He looks

31

a sight, but be thankful for small mercies. He might have wanted to wear a space suit with an oversize goldfish bowl as headpiece. At least I'm spared the risk of a tear in his best flannel shorts." She called over her shoulder, "Are you ready, John?"

"Just coming."

There was the sound of a bolt on the kitchen door slipping into place, and a moment later their father appeared. For a moment he looked at his younger son in dismay, then with a good-humoured gesture that sent the large, wide-brimmed hat toppling over the boy's eyes, he said, "So you thought you'd introduce the pioneering touch, did you? Well, here's to the wide open spaces. Lead on, Six-Shooter-Sam."

3 . . . *The Interview*

THE TRAIN sped on through the countryside, where the meadows seemed like green silk shot through with threads of gold. Paul, who soon tired of his self-invented game of spotting black sheep among the white, decided that he was hungry, and his mother, realizing that it might be wiser to have lunch before the interview, handed around some of the sandwiches. The children ate theirs with every sign of enjoyment, but their father seemed to have difficulty in swallowing so much as a mouthful. His wife looked at him in affectionate concern.

"What's the matter, dear? Have I put too much mustard on the ham?"

"Dad's suffering from a going-to-the-dentist sort of feeling," remarked Ian, biting noisily into an apple.

"Are you, Dad?" Paul was astonished to think that a grownup might be human enough to feel nervous. "Is your tummy full of butterflies? Do let me listen."

Ian tugged him back by his bright yellow scarf.

"No, it isn't," replied his father, "but it *is* telling me I must be crazy giving into you all as I have done. It might help, Lee, if you told me what you wrote."

Ian laughed. "It isn't difficult to guess. Knowing Lee, I'd say she probably went all Jane Austenish as she does sometimes in her journal and told Mr. Clevedon how much you were longing to break out of your prison, and how much her dear brothers would benefit from good country air."

Leonie pinched him.

"Hi! Lay off! That hurt."

"It was meant to. If you must know, I didn't mention either of you because I didn't want to spoil Daddy's chances."

"Then how did you explain yourself? You must have signed the letter," continued her logical brother. "Or did you add forgery to your other talents?" He looked at her and gave a low whistle. "You're a cool customer, using Dad's name."

His sister's pale cheeks flushed.

"I didn't. I . . . I . . . used Mummy's name and said that I was writing on behalf of Mr. John Meredith."

Ian rolled his eyes in an exaggerated look of dismay.

"We have a crook in the family."

"Good," said Paul. "That makes us more interesting." He turned to his sister. "Don't worry, Lee. I don't suppose you'll get more than five years, if Mr. Clevedon decides to persecute."

34

"Prosecute, you idiot," corrected his brother.

Leonie, however, was not heeding either of them. Sheltered behind the barrier of her own thoughts, she spent the next half-hour building up an imaginary picture of the man they were going to meet. He would be genial, and a little on the stout side, she decided, with tiny, crinkly lines of laughter round his eyes, and nothing but praise for her father's courage in applying for the job. And if ever her part in the plan came to light, some of the praise would be hers. "How lucky you are to have a daughter like Leonie," he would say. "If it hadn't been for her we should never have met, and this beautiful old place of mine might have gone to rack and ruin." Leonie felt a warm tide of pleasure washing over her, but because she wanted no one to think her vain or swollen-headed, she modestly lowered her gaze to the floor.

"I should jolly well think you ought to hang your head in shame," said Paul, returning to the attack. "Do they let you have visits in prison, Dad?"

Leonie came to herself with a start, to hear her father telling Paul to be quiet and to see her mother stuffing sandwich papers and apple cores into a bag. A quarter of an hour later the train came to a standstill in Mapledon Station. Mr. Meredith got out first, and with his family following hard upon his heels, strode along the platform.

The ticket collector, whose duties combined those of stationmaster and porter, watched them with a contemplative eye. Few passengers alighted at his sleepy, unimportant station, and those that did never failed to rouse his interest.

Before he could accept the outgoing halves of their tickets, an elderly lady tugged at his sleeve. She wore a finely knitted sweater set, much darned at the elbows, and a tweed skirt that reached almost to her ankles. Under the wide, floppy brim of her straw hat, her eyes had the patient, inquiring look of a child and her skin, drawn tightly back from the patrician nose and gently curving mouth, had the downy bloom of a peach.

"Bassett!" she began. "Don't tell me that my parcel hasn't come by this train. Dear me. How very tiresome. Now I shall have nothing to read over the weekend. If only some public-spirited person would start a lending library in Mapledon, how grateful we old folks would be."

Leonie felt her sympathy stir. It must be awful to be old and disappointed, she thought. Acting on an impulse, she pointed to a paper-back novel sticking out of the picnic basket.

"We have a thriller if you would like to have it," she began shyly. "Daddy says he won't read it now, because I've spoiled the suspense by accidentally letting out who did the dastardly deed."

The old lady looked surprised and pleased.

"How very kind of you, my dear. If you're sure your father can spare it, I should be most grateful." Mr. Meredith, amused not to be spoken to directly, surrendered the book willingly. The old lady glanced at the title. "*Shroud for Susannah*—sounds deliciously sinister."

"It is," said Leonie. "It's all about a girl who . . ."

Ian clapped a hand over her mouth.

"There you go again." He grinned at the old lady. "She can't help it."

The old lady smiled back. "I sympathize with her. My

tongue used to run away with me when I was a girl. It hasn't so many opportunities now."

"Haven't you many friends?" asked Paul.

"Course Miss Tracy has," declared the stationmaster. "Any amount, only she's that independent."

"That will do, Bassett," she broke in. "These young people here have far more exciting things to do than listen to you airing my shortcomings."

"Exciting!" Bassett sucked in the ends of his drooping moustache. "I wouldn't call Mapledon exciting since your brother died, unless, of course you count the Major's feud with the villagers."

Miss Tracy made clucking noises with her tongue.

"I have said that will do, Bassett," she repeated, in a much more imperious tone. "Our village troubles have nothing to do with this gentleman, who I can see is becoming increasingly impatient to be off. So take their tickets, and let them enjoy their picnic in our lovely Mapledon woods."

"On the contrary, I want Mappins . . . Mr. Clevedon's place," replied Mr. Meredith, glad indeed to think that his release was imminent. "I should be grateful if you could tell me how to get there."

Bassett pushed his peaked cap to the back of his head and scratched his thick, wiry hair.

"Well! If that don't beat the band. Your Mr. Clevedon is our Major, the chap we was a-talking of." He would have asked questions, but a look from the old lady quelled his curiosity.

"How fortunate then that I happened to come to the station. Mappins was once my home." With a brief nod in the stationmaster's direction, she led the way through the diminutive ticket office and turned right in the direction of the village High Street. "I fear me, you will find the place sadly changed," she went on. "My brother took a great interest in the life of this village. But opening up the gardens for cricket matches, fêtes, Sunday-school outings and garden parties didn't help pay the taxes." Her voice faltered. "I . . . I . . . did my best to keep up the old traditions when he died, but, alas, it was no good. A year ago, although it nearly broke my heart, I sold everything."

"And the Major doesn't carry on the good work. Is that what Bassett meant by a feud?" asked Ian.

Miss Tracy shielded her face from the heat of the sun by dragging the brim of her hat even lower over her eyes.

"I suppose so, but I am afraid I know very little about the Major. You see, all the details of the sale were conducted between our two solicitors, and so far only Gregg, he's the Major's manservant, has crossed my threshold." She hesitated, then went on. "Naturally in a small place like Mapledon there is gossip and rumors fly as fast as crows."

"What sort of rumors?" asked Ian.

"Chiefly that the Major has allowed certain disadvantages to turn him into a rather bitter man." She paused again. "But what am I saying? As friends of his, you must know all this and more."

"We aren't friends of his, at least not yet," said Paul indiscreetly. "Daddy's come down to apply for the job of estate manager."

"Paul!" exclaimed his father, with justifiable irritation.

"Please don't scold him," begged Miss Tracy. "The

news delights me. That's what the place needs. A young family and new ideas." Her short, tripping steps halted. "Now this is where I turn off to my cottage. From here the way to Mappins is quite straightforward. Climb the hill beside the church and at the top you will see a stile and a footpath. Follow it across the field and within ten minutes of leaving a small copse you will come to the main garden and the house." Mr. Meredith thanked her. Miss Tracy waved a hand. "Good luck to you, and if, as Mr. Parkes would say, you find the Major so full of crotchets and quavers you could play him on the piano, don't be discouraged."

"What did she mean by that?" asked Paul, as with a last wave of farewell they left the village and began climbing the hill.

"I imagine it was her own odd way of saying he was a tough nut to crack," replied his father.

Ian looked over his shoulder.

"I'm beginning to hope he's too tough." Fresh from the crowded canvas of a London suburb, he had no eyes for the old-world charm and dignity of the village, nestling within the protective shadow of the church. "Did you ever see such miserable little shops? And not even a movie or a community center to liven things up. What on earth do people find to do in such a dump?"

Paul looked about him too.

"There's one good thing. I couldn't see a school, so perhaps you don't have to worry about eleven-plus exams down here."

His father quickly put him straight.

"Sorry to disappoint you, Paul. If you'd kept your eyes

open, you'd have seen the school-bus collecting point marked up on the wall adjoining the butcher's shop."

Silenced by this remark, Paul breasted the brow of the hill, climbed the stile Miss Tracy had indicated, then ran along the narrow footpath. To the right, where the field of pale gold wheat sloped downwards to the valley, he caught a glimpse of water. To the left, beyond the boundary hedge, close-knit ranks of elm and oak stood darkly green against the blue sky. From them came the noisy orchestration of rooks. Arrested by the sound, he fitted a strip of caps into his pistol and fired three shots high into the air. The brittle reports died away, and as the birds rose in a black-winged cloud, he was filled with delight.

"I'll be a rook and jay scarer-offer," he announced, rushing back to his father. "And when I've earned enough money, I'll buy a horse. Perhaps I won't have to buy one. Perhaps the Major's got lots of horses."

Excited by this new possibility he raced ahead again, entered the thin, straggling copse and emerged to enjoy his first glimpse of the house. Tall chimneys dominated the gray slate roof. The windows were wide, and the red brick walls almost concealed by creeper. If the house had mellowed with age, the gardens had not. Where the terrace ended and the formal garden began, it was difficult to tell which were flowers and which were weeds, so tangled was the encroachment of grass and thistles.

When the rest of the family caught up with him, no one spoke for a few moments; then, with a barely perceptible bracing of his shoulders, Mr. Meredith said, "So that is Mappins. What do you think of it, Ellen?"

"Not as large as I'd imagined, the house, I mean. But

40

it's a little frightening. It looks so shuttered, so uncared for. What a wilderness of a garden!"

Her husband linked his arm in hers.

"Say the word, and we'll go no further,"

"I may be frightened, but I'm also curious."

With a warning to the children not to go too far and to be sure and return within an hour or so, she and Mr. Meredith walked slowly toward the house.

"Let's explore the wood," said Paul. "I bet I can climb trees faster than you can."

Ian did not accept the challenge, but accompanied his sister along another path, skirting the copse, which led them to the stream. A solitary fisherman, wearing a checked cap, and a townsman's jacket over trousers rolled up above the ankles, waded in the shallows. The unsuitable attire, and his awkward gestures, struck both young people at once. He looked about as out of place as a shark in a goldfish bowl. Nevertheless, being friendly, they approached him.

"Good morning, or rather, good afternoon," said Leonie politely. "Have you caught much?"

The man climbed the bank and searched for bait in a dirty, crumpled green handkerchief.

"Nary a one," he replied, looking up at her from beneath the brim of his greasy cap. "Too much pesky sunshine. A bit of mist and a hint of rain, and you can almost pick 'em out of the water with your bare hands."

"Do you live in the village?" asked Ian.

The man spat in the water.

"Me, live in that dead and alive hole! Not likely. My home's in London."

Ian looked puzzled.

41

"Then how do you come to be fishing here?" Glancing along the path he saw a board bearing the words *Fishing Prohibited*. The man followed his gaze and laughed.

"Oh, I'm not blind, but I'm a sucker for the old saying, 'What the eye don't see, the 'eart don't grieve about.' Not that the Major's got much 'eart for anything. My fishing's no secret from Gregg, though."

"Who is Gregg?" asked Leonie, forgetting Miss Tracy's earlier mention of him. "He isn't the new estate manager, is he?"

The man gave a derisive chuckle.

"Estate manager! That's a good one. Bless you, Gregg don't know a dock leaf from a dandelion. He looks after the Major. Helpless as a babe in arms he'd be without him. And well the old so-and-so knows it." He cackled again. "Suits us, though. Me and Gregg know how to line our nests with a feather or two. Serves Major Clevedon right, the sour-faced, sour-tongued old devil."

"It doesn't sound very honest," said Leonie.

"Honest! What's honesty got to do with it? If the Major chooses to play the hermit, why shouldn't we take what pickings we can?" All at once his friendliness changed to suspicion. " 'Old 'ard a minute. You're asking a mighty lot of questions. Where do you come from?"

"London," replied Leonie.

"So that's the way of the wind, it is? You let the cat out of the bag when you spoke of an estate manager. Your Dad's after the job, isn't he?" Leonie nodded, then fell back as the man took a step toward her. "Then see here, Missy. One squeak about all this, and you and your cock sparrow of a brother will be sorry you ever set foot in the place. Not that your father'll take on the job, if he's got as much sense as the others."

Leonie backed still further away, but Ian stood his ground. He suddenly saw the man for what he was, not a harmless fisherman but a shifty, dirty ne'er-do-well.

"Don't think you can frighten me with your threats. If Dad does get the job, he'll jolly well see that there's no more poaching. A well-stocked stream means money."

"So you'd squeal on me, would you . . . you miserable, pasty-faced brat." Stooping he picked up a stone, but before he could right himself and take aim, Ian darted forward and shooting out a foot tripped him. With a cry that was half fury, half fright, the man teetered on the edge of the bank, then fell with a resounding splash into the water. Leonie took to her heels and ran. Ian walked slowly and did not look back. At a bend in the path he caught up with his sister. "He won't drown, will he?" she asked apprehensively.

"In fifteen inches of water! Not a hope. All he'll get is a wetting and serve him right. Five feet six of nastiness, that's what he is."

His sister's look was full of admiration.

"You were terribly brave. I was shaking in my shoes all the time."

"Cut it out, Lee." Ian grabbed her by the hand. "Come on. Let's find the other gangster."

The wood was denser than they had imagined, and from the quiet behavior of the birds, it was plain that Paul was nowhere in the vicinity. Ian transferred his search to another stretch of the stream, leaving his sister to scan the nearby meadows. When they met again half an hour later, neither had been successful. Leonie began to feel anxious. There was no knowing where Paul might be, or worse still, what he might be doing.

"Are you certain he wasn't anywhere along the bank of the stream? It's much deeper where you were looking. Suppose he had fallen in."

"Stop panicking," replied her brother. "You're the only non-swimmer in the family. Paul swims like a fish."

"Not with all his clothes on."

"If I know Paul, he's probably in the kitchen wheedling buns out of Gregg."

"Gregg doesn't sound like the sort of person to give away buns," Leonie said, agreeing nevertheless that the only sensible thing to do was to return to the house.

As they approached the terrace they saw that their father and mother were not alone. Beside them, sitting in a wheel chair with a rug across his knees, was a thick-set, broad-shouldered man. His face wore an expression of angry pride, which had somehow become permanently twisted into a mold of hostility. As Leonie gazed at the sharply chiseled features and met the coldness of his eyes, she felt a shiver run down her spine. If this was the Major, she hoped her father had failed.

"These are two of your handicaps, I presume," he began, addressing Mr. Meredith. "Where is the third?"

"Vanished into thin air," replied Ian promptly. Unlike his sister he was never intimidated or tongue-tied in the presence of strangers. "And it's not a bit of use blaming us, Mother, or telling us to search. We've looked in all the likely places already."

44

"Oh dear! How could Paul be so tiresome?" His mother was plainly embarrassed. "I'm so sorry, Major, but I'm afraid we shall have to trespass upon your patience until he does turn up."

Ian swung around.

"You're the Major!"

"You sound surprised."

"I am a bit."

"And shocked, no doubt, to find I'm a helpless cripple."

"Not shocked . . . only . . ." Ian never completed his sentence.

At that moment there was a scuffle at the far end of the terrace. In the next instant Paul appeared, held in the grip of a tall weather-hardened countryman. At the sight of his parents he made another effort, and breaking free, ran toward them. The cowboy hat hung around his neck; dirt streaked his face and his hands.

"Don't listen to him. I wasn't doing any harm," he shouted. "I wasn't."

"What is the trouble, Parkes?" asked the Major, before Mrs. Meredith could utter a word. "No, on second thought, let the boy speak."

Paul shot him a grateful look, then spying the wheel chair with its simple moter fixed above the front wheels, his eyes glinted.

"I say! That's a smashing thing to ride about in. I bet you fairly whizz down the lanes."

"I seldom whizz anywhere," replied the Major dryly. "Do you know who I am?"

"Of course I do. Mr. Parkes told me. You're the Major. You've lost the use of your legs and you own Mappins." He looked again at the chair. "I bet I could race you. I won the hundred yards in record time at school."

For the first time a hint of amusement softened the Major's harsh expression, but only for a moment.

"We seem to have wandered from the point, young man," he said coldly.

"I was hoping we wouldn't have to come back to it." Paul's frankness was engaging. "Mr. Parkes said you'd skin me alive when you knew."

"It was like this, sir," broke in the farmer. "I caught this youngster red-handed tormenting your old horse. Flinging a rope at him, he was, the young devil."

Paul was indignant.

"I wasn't tormenting him. I was trying to lasso him like the cowboys do on television. I found the rope in a field."

"And you need a taste of it on your backside," continued the farmer. "You town kids are all alike. Got no more sense in your heads than a scarecrow has."

"It isn't like you to be cruel," said his mother.

Paul's eyes opened wider and wider to prevent the pricking tears from falling.

"I wasn't being cruel. He was bored and lonely until I came. I . . . I . . . did all the right things like letting him smell the rope and get the feel of it around his neck before I threw it, and he was enjoying it. I know he was from the way he tossed his head and whinnied every time I missed. Then Mr. Parkes had to come along and spoil everything." His eyes became wistful. "Gosh! That horse is a beauty, even if he is old and a pensioner. Do you think I could ride him sometimes when we come to live here?"

46

"There isn't any possibility of that," declared his father. "Major Clevedon considers you children three too many, and having listened to you, I'm inclined to agree with him. I apologize for my son, Major." There was regret and disappointment in his voice, but nonetheless a determination to be gone. "Now before anyone else gets into mischief, we'd better go."

"And how do you propose getting back to London?" inquired the Major.

"As we came. By train, of course."

Major Clevedon glanced at his wristwatch.

"You should have made fuller use of the timetable before you set out. This is a small branch line and the last train left exactly five minutes ago. So unless you prefer to spend the night on the platform waiting for the milk train, I suggest you accept the hospitality of my roof for one night at least."

4 . . . *Misadventure in the Night*

IN THE small bedroom on the second floor of the house Paul
tossed and turned on his narrow bed. The mattress was lumpy,
and try as he would to keep the sheet uppermost, the blanket
would keep tickling his chin. To add to his discomfort he
was conscious of a dull pain in the pit of his stomach.

He tried to forget it by dwelling on the beautiful gray
horse he had made friends with on Mr. Parkes's farm. It was
a prince of a horse. With its flying mane and long tail, it reminded him again of the one the Queen had ridden during
the Trooping the Color. Yet even though he visualized himself astride it, leaping hedges and gates in magnificent style,
the uncomfortable pain in his stomach persisted.

48

Now more than ever he regretted eating the supper Gregg had provided. But Gregg had been so anxious to please, and so sorry that his father had not succeeded in getting the job, that he had not had the heart to refuse a helping of the indigestible, pasty pie.

Paul groaned aloud. Feeling that a drink might help, he got out of bed, rolled up the too-long legs of his borrowed pyjamas, and with a blanket draped around his shoulders, went in search of the bathroom.

Once he was in the long, dark corridor, his sense of direction failed him. There were so many doors, and he had no wish to disturb his parents. With the folds of the blanket gathered more closely about him he went downstairs to try to find the kitchen. The hall was a well of darkness broken only by a thin edge of light showing beneath one of

the doors. This couldn't be the kitchen, he knew, but perhaps Gregg slept on the ground floor. And Gregg would be able to help him. There was no response to his knock, and when he peered around the door he found that it was the Major's bedroom. To his surprise the room was empty.

Going to the window, he drew aside the heavy curtain and peered out. The fineness of the day had given way to a thin drizzle, and this made the Major's disappearance even more puzzling. Allowing the curtain to fall into place, he caught sight of a glass of milk standing on a low table. At once he was reminded of his thirst and his stomach ache. Reluctant to wander further, he sat on a chair and drank half of it. The milk was cool and of a strange flavor, but it was refreshing.

For a few moments he sat where he was, taking stock of the neat room with everything precisely in its place, then as he put the glass back on the table he noticed an open notebook. One page was blank, but on the other, in a neat script, was a list of names. Paul did not mean to pry, but he was surprised to find Miss Tracy's name among them, and he picked the book up. All at once the letters began behaving strangely. They were no longer black and clear, but blurred and dancing all over the page. He rubbed his eyes, replaced the book and tottered unsteadily toward the door. He never reached it, for with the floor appearing to come up and hit him, he fell in a heap on the bed.

He awoke eight hours later to find himself covered with his own comforter. His head and his eyelids felt weighted, and the discomfort in his stomach was, if anything, worse. Nevertheless he tried to sit up and remember. As he did so,

50

a stranger leaned over the tall bedpost at the foot of the bed and smiled to him.

"So you've wakened up at last. A fine young scallywag you were to drag me away from my well-earned rest. Your mother's been half frantic with worry, and I've only this minute persuaded her to go and get something to eat."

Paul blinked in the strong mid-morning sunshine.

"Are you a doctor?"

"Yes, I'm Dr. Bailey." He felt Paul's pulse with one hand and picked up the half-empty glass with the other. "Perhaps you will explain how you came to drink a sleeping potion intended for the Major?"

Little by little the events of the night came back and Paul related them as clearly as he could. At the end he said, "Does the Major often go out at night?"

"I couldn't say," Dr. Bailey replied. "I've only been to the house twice and both times on your account. The Major was the one to find you, you know. He was scared out of his wits. Didn't you notice that the milk had an unusual flavor?"

"Yes, I suppose I did. But I told you, I had a pain and I was thirsty."

"How do you feel now?"

Paul thought quickly.

"Awful. And it's mostly Gregg's fault. He's a dreadful cook. You could knock his pastry sky high and it still wouldn't break."

Dr. Bailey pushed his patient back onto the pillow, pulled up the oversize pyjama jacket and pressed gently in the area of the boy's abdomen. Paul winced and groaned at the wrong moments. The doctor gave him a shrewd glance.

"I don't think there's anything wrong with you but an oversize bout of indigestion."

Paul appraised him through narrowed eyelids.

"You couldn't by any chance call it a grumbling appendix, could you?"

"You should study anatomy a bit more." The doctor chuckled. "Your appendix is way down south. Come on. Own up. What was behind those agonized groans?"

"Promise you won't give me away if I tell you?"

The promise given, Dr. Bailey listened attentively to the story he was told.

"At first, I thought Lee's idea was daft. She is a bit off the beam at times, you know. All girls are. But I hadn't had a chance to explore Mappins then, and now I have, I like it. There are ravens and magpies in the wood, and a whopping great woodpecker as well. He's the fellow that plays drums on the bark of a tree." His puppy face lit up. "And there's a most wonderful horse, an exciting, tumbledown boathouse, and a stream that sings to you which is absolutely teeming with fish." He paused, took a deep breath, and finally came to the point. "So you see, Doctor, if you weren't satisfied with my condition. I couldn't be moved, could I? And that would mean that Daddy, Mummy and the others couldn't go either. A lot of things could happen before I got better."

Dr. Bailey tried to look stern.

"Young man! Do you know what you're asking me to do?"

Paul nodded. "I expect I do, but I have got a truly, truly sort of pain, and it would be a truly worthwhile sort of half fib."

52

"I ought not to say so, but I'm inclined to agree with you." Dr. Bailey unhooked the stethoscope from his neck. "Mappins needs a bit of young life about the place. So does the Major, although he'd be the last to admit it. He had a fine army record, you know."

"Was that when he was wounded?"

Dr. Bailey snapped the locks of his medical case.

"No, he came through the war without a scratch. I've been interested in him ever since he came here, but it was old Miss Tracy who told me something of what happened."

Paul clasped his bony fingers around his knees. "What did happen?"

"He had an unlucky accident while rock climbing. A wrong handhold in failing light dislodged a fall of rock. The Major fell and was buried beneath a minor avalanche."

"How awful!" Paul's eyes widened. "Won't he ever be able to walk again?"

The doctor shook his head.

"I'm afraid not. But even if he is chained to a wheel chair for the rest of his life, there's still a good deal he could do and share."

Paul nodded. "That's what I think." His brown eyes, which at times could be as appealing as a spaniel's, went to work on the doctor. "Are you going to be a sport and work things for me?"

Dr. Bailey's eyes twinkled. "You'll bring an awful lot of punishment down on your head if I do. I can't agree to a grumbling appendix, but whatever I decide upon will have to be treated with the utmost respect. You won't be able to eat solid food for a bit and you won't be able to run about."

At this threat to his liberty, Paul's face sobered. Then,

as suddenly, it broke into smiles as he saw that the wheel chair was back in its customary position against the wall.

"I could be pushed around in one of those. The Major's got two."

"You could, if I can persuade the Major of the gravity of your case, and at the same time allay your mother's fears."

"You'll manage," Paul assured him. "Doctors always have plenty of initiation."

Smiling at the boy's unlucky vocabulary, Dr. Bailey closed the bedroom door behind him and went in search of the rest of the family. Paul lay back, a look of triumph on his face.

"Good old Gregg," he murmured to himself, patting his midriff. "And good old tummy. Mind you don't get better too soon."

Five minutes later his mother and father entered the room. Both looked concerned.

"Is the pain very bad?" his mother asked.

"I can't hear it grumbling at the moment," Paul answered, "but I expect it will if I move. Still I must, mustn't I, because you want to get home as soon as possible." With an expression of bravely-borne suffering he tried to rise, but his mother restrained him.

"You're not to move, dear. What with the Major finding you lying in a drugged sleep, we've been scared enough." Her usually serene face became suddenly angry. "I can't think why he wanted to go out in the night. If he couldn't sleep, why didn't he drink the beastly stuff? If he had, you would have been spared this acute acidity disorder."

"Is that what I've got?" Paul applauded the doctor's cleverness.

54

"And let it be a lesson to you," broke in his father. "Anything in a glass not specifically poured out for you is strictly taboo in future. And milk of all things. When I think of the coaxing and indecent bribery that goes on at home in order to get you to down a half pint, I give up."

"You drink anything when you're thirsty and have a pain." Paul's voice became a little sulky. He was not getting the sympathy he thought he deserved. "I . . . I . . . might have died, you know."

"Don't." His mother put a hand to his forehead. "I can't bear to think about it. I only wish we could get you home, instead of having to stay on here in a stranger's house."

This was better. Paul brightened, then reverted to his wan expression.

"Are we staying on for long?"

"Yes, we are, Paul." His father seemed momentarily at a loss for words. "I . . . I . . . don't know whether to be pleased or not. As you know, I didn't take my full vacation last year. I've phoned my manager at home and he's agreed to let me add a week. That gives me a month. The Major has suggested that I spend the time making plans and suggestions for improving the property."

"Hurrah!" Paul said this with such vigor that he at once aroused suspicion. "It's all right, Dad," he continued. "That was my last fling." With his cheeks fast becoming pale and his voice a wail, he added, "Mummy! I feel sick."

Paul's genuine disability lasted well into the afternoon, and he was glad to be carried up to his own bedroom. By the early evening, however, the bilious attack was over, and when Leonie and Ian appeared with a tray bearing a bowl of soup and crisp toast, he ate with good appetite.

"Easy to tell this isn't Gregg's brew," he said, smacking his lips. "This is Mummy's."

"You're right, it is," replied his sister. "She's already worked wonders in the kitchen and had poor old Gregg running round in circles."

"What did you have for supper?"

"Soup, cutlets and tomatoes, followed by one of Mum's gorgeous trifles," answered Ian. "And don't put on your martyred expression. You brought this bowl of slop on yourself, fathead."

Paul pushed away the tray. "What do you mean?" He still felt hungry, and at the thought of what he had missed, his mouth filled with saliva.

"I mean, you may be able to pull the wool over Mum and Dad's eyes, but not over ours. All right. We know you've been sick. I've never heard such disgusting noises. But anyone would be after being cloddish enough to swallow an adult sleeping draught. And your appendix isn't so much as murmuring. Still, if we can ginger up the place a bit, it might be a jolly good plan, and the doctor's a sport to aid and abet it."

Paul gave him a withering look.

"You aren't being clever. He never said anything about my appendix talking. It's my tummy. It's turned to an acid drop. You listened outside the door."

Leonie confessed that they had.

"We didn't mean to eavesdrop. We were honestly worried."

"Then, as you know, you can jolly well go downstairs and smuggle me up some bread and cheese and a large apple," said Paul, adding with relish that they would both have to share his self-inflicted punishment by taking him out for airings in the wheel chair. "I'm not allowed to put a foot to the ground for days and days."

"That's what you think," said Ian, but he went docilely enough to see what further sustenance the larder had to offer. When he returned a few minutes later, the plate held nothing but a large wedge of cake. Paul grumbled, and as he ate, watched his brother turning over the sheets of the local newspaper. Within a moment or so he tossed them onto the floor.

"Heavens! What a one-eyed hole this must be. Do you know how much news value Mapledon has? One small paragraph on the back page devoted to a Mrs. Marshall celebrating her hundredth birthday. And all she can find to say is that Mapledon isn't what it was, and that she doesn't want to see another birthday."

"And she's right," said Paul. "But it wasn't dull before the Major took over Mappins." He paused and became thoughtful. "I wonder if we could do anything about it. A month isn't a very long time."

5 . . . *A Fishy Lunch*

THERE WAS no opportunity to talk any longer, for at that moment their mother's footsteps could be heard along the uncarpeted corridor. Paul pushed the crumby plate under his pillow, and with a chameleon-like aptitude for changing color, assumed his look of frailty.

"Now, no more talking, darling," she began, turning a reproachful look on the others. "Really, Ian. I thought you would have had more sense than to tire him after such a bad bout. He looks exhausted."

Paul looked even more wan. Ian scowled, and fearing an outburst, Leonie dragged him from the room.

Next morning their younger brother awoke refreshed and eager to begin the day. Then, as his feet shrank from the cold touch of the linoleum and a cheerful whistle broke from his lips, he remembered. He was supposed to be an invalid, and an invalid neither whistled nor got up for breakfast. In the nick of time he took a flying leap back into bed, and had just arranged the tumbled bedclothes when Gregg entered carrying a tray. Behind him, as close as his own shadow, came Leonie and Ian.

Gregg was of medium height and moved with the springy step of a boxer. His flat, almost bridgeless nose and obtruding ears heightened that impression, but his hands did not. They were small and surprisingly neat-fingered. For a second or so he stood looking down at the boy, then his lips parted to reveal the ugly gap left by a missing tooth.

"Well. 'Ow do you feel now? Perky or pernickety?"

"I feel . . ." Paul had been about to say "fine," but again he remembered in time. "I feel as well as can be expected in the circumstances."

"Then dig into this stuff." Gregg placed the tray across his knees and watched while Paul took the top off his egg. Suddenly he let out a wail.

"It isn't cooked. I hate runny eggs."

"For goodness' sake, pipe down," said Ian. "Mix it all up together. If you don't eat it, Mother won't let you get up at all today."

Paul scowled, poured out the watery white and dipped a finger of thin bread and butter into the yolk. Then he brightened as he remembered the wheel chair.

"You could push me to the stream," he said, "and perhaps we could fish. You'd like some freshly caught fish for supper, wouldn't you, Gregg?"

Ian made the most of the opportunity.

59

"It wouldn't be a treat for Gregg. He has his own source of supply."

"And what might you mean by that?"

"Only that we met your poacher friend who told us that he shares his catches with you."

"You mind what you're a-saying of, Master Ian. I don't have no dealings with poachers. 'Twould be more than my job's worth. 'Alf a mo', though. What was this fellow like?" Ian described him. "I thought as much. He's a lazy good-for-nothing, who haunts the village picking up what jobs he can. The Major took him on once, but he weren't no good and was soon sent packing. But he was here long enough to get the lie of the land, and being ferret-sharp like, he must have realized that a little fish sold on the sly means easy money. Then you goes and catches him red-handed, and he takes his revenge by making me share the blame." Gregg looked sorrowful. "That's human nature for you, that is."

Ian nodded. The explanation was reasonable enough.

"Oughtn't the Major to be warned?"

"He wouldn't care. The Major ain't interested in anything, more's the pity. You should have seen him when I first caught up with him."

"When was that?" asked Ian.

"Long afore this nipper was thought of," replied Gregg, pointing to Paul. "I was his batman during the war. Now make no mistake, war's a terrible thing, but for me, them were the days. When peace came, he went his way and I went mine. Then, when I was a bit down on me uppers, I sees an advertisement in a paper. 'Greggy boy,' I says to meself, 'if this Major Clevedon is the one you did a bit of spit

60

and polish for, then you're in clover.' And he was, although, mind you, you could'ave knocked me down with a feather when I first sees him hunched in his chair and all the old spirit knocked out of him."

"Did he talk much about himself?" asked Leonie.

"Not him. And I kept mum, too. You don't ask questions of the Major if you know what's good for you. And he didn't ask none of me either, which suited yours truly." Gregg moved toward the door, then turned. "Blow me down, if I haven't forgotten to give you this."

Fumbling in his pocket, he brought out a crumpled letter. Ian took it, and when Gregg had gone, slit the envelope.

Dear Ian, he read aloud,

I am addressing you as the oldest of the trio. Although circumstances have persuaded me to extend my hospitality, I think you should know that I am in no way reconciled to the idea of having children about the place.

In fact Paul's intrusion into my bedroom, with disastrous consequences to himself, only confirms my belief that modern children are bad mannered and meddlesome. If this judgment seems harsh, the greasy thumb-mark on my notebook is further proof.

My one consolation is that the gardens are large enough to put distance between us. So while you are free to roam as you will, and entertain yourselves as best you may while your father thinks up ways of restoring my property, you will avoid my ground-floor rooms, and thus allow me the privacy I desire.

Brett Clevedon

P.S.—Since Dr. Bailey takes a more serious view of Paul's indisposition than I do, your brother may have the occasional use of my second wheel chair until he is fit to use his own legs.

Ian folded the letter.

"Pleasant little missive, isn't it?" he said sarcastically. "Just adds that extra ray of sunshine to the day!" He turned on his brother. "Perhaps now you'll remember to wash your hands before going to bed, you mucky little pup. Seems to me you are becoming a Paul Pry. What on earth possessed you to pick up his miserable old book?"

"I don't know," replied Paul, now completely subdued. "Perhaps because I was surprised to see Miss Tracy's name written down. Hers didn't have a check by it as some of the others did. But if the Major never goes out and never meets anyone, why should he make a sort of visiting list?"

"Search me," said his brother. "It could be part of the feud Bassett spoke about. Perhaps the Major amuses himself by writing rude letters." He screwed up the one he had received. "He's pretty good at them. He might even write them anonymously. Anything else in the book to suggest a motive?"

Paul shook his head. "I only looked for a minute, then the letters started to go wobbly." Paul was badly hurt by the Major's opinion of him, and tears again pricked at his eyes. "I'm not a Paul Pry, and I didn't mean to be meddlesome; now that the Major's angry, everything's horrid. I want to go home."

Leonie put her arms around him and hugged him.

"Don't cry, Paul."

"I'm not crying." He wriggled free of her embrace. "I've . . . I've got something in my eye. Mummy's right," he went on, with a return of his usual spirits. "None of this would have happened if the Major hadn't gone out late at night.

"You've got something there," murmured Ian. "A very odd habit, prowling about in the dark, like a bat."

"He doesn't prowl," protested Leonie. "He propels himself around in his chair."

"How can you be sure of that?" demanded Ian, determined to bring a bit of excitement into the day. His voice became sinister. "Supposing he isn't really a cripple, but leading a sort of Jekyll-and-Hyde existence. Darkness can cover many a dastardly deed. Who knows? Perhaps Miss Tracy is next on the list."

Leonie did not like the turn the conversation had taken. When Ian started talking like a third-rate film script there was no knowing where his imagination would lead him.

"Shut up," she said, observing that Paul was drinking in every word. "The Major may be sour tempered, but he's no character out of a thriller. Why, the very house has been altered to help him move about more easily. You ought to be ashamed of yourself."

Ian slouched to the window and stared down at Gregg, who was burning refuse.

"All right, Lee. Cut the sermon. I only said it to liven up Paul a bit." He yawned loudly. "Ye gods and little fishes! What does one do in a hole such as this? I've a good mind to go and help Gregg."

His sister picked up the tray.

"I should. It might help to get rid of your flabbiness."

Ian turned on her, indigation in every line of his face. "What did you say?"

"That you're a flab, flab, flabby."

Ian went for her, and as Lee ducked, the tray went flying. The milk Paul had refused to drink shot from the glass and cascaded down his forehead. The china scattered itself in broken pieces about the linoleum. The accident sobered them all.

"Guilty," said Leonie.

"Guilty," said Ian.

"Not guilty," said Paul, "so perhaps one of you will mop me up."

Half an hour later, still hungry but dressed, he allowed himself to be helped down the broad curve of the staircase. Ian, who had been scolded by Gregg for the breakfast breakages, gave that help none too gently and earned a further reproof from his mother, who stood in the hall dressed in her outdoor things.

"Are you going for a walk, too?" asked Paul.

"I'm going home." Mrs. Meredith ran a finger down a timetable. "As there's been such a drastic change in our plans, I must cancel milk and newspapers, collect more clothes and make arrangements for Mr. Smithers. I do hope the poor thing won't lose his appetite and pine. Still, we can always fatten him up again on cod-liver oil."

"He can have all my milk," Paul said generously, wishing in the next instant that he had never mentioned the word.

"Did you drink yours this morning?"

"I licked up quite a lot."

"That's good," his mother went on, her thoughts already

64

halfway to London. "Now let me see. I think I've thought of most things. Gregg has cut you some sandwiches, and I've poured some soup into a thermos flask for Paul, so you can all spend the day out in this lovely sunshine. Fortunately the Major's taking your father round the estate this morning, and won't be needing his indoor chair."

The goodbyes over, Leonie collected the food from the kitchen, and on going out to the terrace found her younger brother seated and eager to be off.

"Forward, James," he commanded, giving Ian a mischievous glance over his shoulder.

Ian set the chair in motion with a jerk that nearly unseated his brother.

"If you think I'm going to push you around all day, you're mistaken. Once away from the house you walk, or push it yourself."

"Oh no. I don't," retorted Paul. "That would be cheating. A good actor has to play his part all the time. If someone should see me and tell Gregg or the Major, they'd know my tummy was better, then Dr. Bailey might get into trouble, Dad wouldn't get his chance and we'd all be sent home."

"All right. All right."

"And as I'm an invalid, you'll have to indulge my every whim," continued Paul, in his most plaguing manner.

"I'll duck you in the stream, if you don't stop. If I've got to push, you'll go where I want to go."

Ian's preference was for the stream, but when they approached and he saw his father in close consultation with the Major, he changed course abruptly and took the path leading more directly to the village.

Leonie did not mind where she went, provided that she

did not come face to face with the owner of Mappins. All at once, as they reached the point where the hill swung steeply down toward the church, Paul leaned forward and shouted. In the next instant he had bounded out of the chair and run towards the ditch.

"What is it?" cried his sister.

"A tortoise. Look, it's got a message painted on its shell. 'If found, return to Windyway, Church Lane.' That's miles away," he added with a look of wonderment on his face.

"Not more than a hundred yards to be precise," said his brother.

"Well, I bet it seemed miles and miles to him," insisted Paul.

Feeling that they had no alternative but to return the truant to its owner, Paul resettled himself in the chair and cradled the animal in his arms. The tortoise regarded him from sleepy eyes, then, as if saying, "Thanks for the lift," tucked in its head.

Ian resumed his pushing, and as the chair gathered speed down the hill, he had all he could do to keep it under control. Leonie did what she could by flinging her weight back, but both were relieved when they were able to turn it into Church Lane.

Windyway was a small gray stone cottage lying back from the lane in the middle of a large garden. Unlike the gardens at Mappins, this one showed every sign of loving care. Floribunda rose bushes bloomed in a profusion of scarlet and pink; the borders of the flower beds were patterned with catmint, snapdragon, candytuft and marigolds. Bees drifted with lazy humming from one sweet-scented flower to another, while from the left, where the neatly pruned fruit trees gave promise of a heavy yield, came the faint, aromatic scent of herbs. Leonie gazed her fill, and for the first time in her life longed to possess a garden of her own. Her attention was distracted by another shout, this time from Ian.

"Heavens above! There's another tortoise and another!"

"Dozens!" squealed Paul, in high glee. "The garden's full of them."

Paul was right. As they looked more intently they could see that the movement among the flowers was not caused by the breeze, but by the thrust of small, rounded, leathery snouts. Leonie opened the wooden gate, and as Ian steered the chair up the flagstone path a woman came from the rear of the house, carrying a bowl of washed lettuce. Even if they had not recognized the faded print dress and the unfashionable length of skirt, the hat would have given its wearer away. This time it was made from raffia and shaped like an oversize dinner plate, blue ribbons tied under the chin holding it in place.

"Miss Tracy!" exclaimed Leonie.

"Now what a pleasant surprise!" said the old lady, spilling a can of weed killer, a pair of pruning shears and some metal name tabs from her apron pocket. "I was only thinking as I washed the food for my family how nice it would be if someone called to see me. Now you've come, which is doubly good, because it means that your father got the job."

Ian picked up the fallen objects and pointing to the label on the can, remarked that it was a good thing the powder was only harmful to fish and not to tortoises. But Miss Tracy did not seem to be listening. As if the very sight of them had filled her with a flurry of excitement, she went on: "You don't know how happy that makes me. Now Mappins will be restored and that poor, misguided man have something to live for." She paused and pointed to Paul. "But what injury has your brother sustained that he, too, has to ride about in that contraption?"

"It's because of me that we're here at all," answered Paul. "I'm getting over a sleeping pill and Gregg's pastry." He gave his brother a look. "It doesn't matter if Miss Tracy knows." Paul told her the whole story and at the end held out the straying tortoise. "We found this pet of yours wandering in the lane. We didn't know it was yours at the time, but we're awfully glad it is."

Miss Tracy took it from him and stroked the leathery head.

"I couldn't count the number of times Samson's been brought back. He's the worst of the lot for straying."

"Do all your tortoises have names?" asked Paul, getting out of the chair. "How do you know which is which?"

"From the markings on the shells. Samson, you observe, has bold markings round the rim." Miss Tracy stooped and picked up another. "Jonah, on the other hand, has a smooth, undecorated shell." She pointed to the bed of cherry pie. "That one is Magog and the one by the syringa bush is Anthony."

"Now all you want is Cleopatra and your family would be complete," said Ian, smiling.

"But I *have* got a Cleopatra. She stays on the mantelpiece in my sitting room. Come in, my dears, and I'll show her to you." Inside the narrow hall, she paused. "How stupid of me. Here have I been telling you all my family's names and I don't know yours."

Introductions over, the children were led into a long room running from front to back of the cottage. Glowing and warm from the sunshine, it was redeemed from shabbiness by lovingly washed chintzes, grass-green curtains and furniture that had been polished to the color of old sherry. Their gaze, however, went at once to the mantelpiece. On the shelf, in company with a gilt clock, was a rock-crystal tortoise with gleaming green stones for eyes.

"Beautiful, isn't it?" said Miss Tracy, allowing Ian to handle it. "It was a gift from my brother shortly before he died . . . a sort of insurance for my future. I . . . I . . . think he knew that the estate would have to be sold to pay death duties and the debts he had incurred."

Hoping that he did not sound impertinent, Ian asked if it were valuable.

"Extremely so, I should imagine. A famous sculptor carved it, and the emerald eyes alone are probably worth many hundreds of pounds."

"Emeralds!" exclaimed Ian.

Miss Tracy nodded. "Not that I think of it in terms of money. Nothing would persuade me to part with it. Cleopatra, together with a few pieces of furniture, is all that I have to remind me of my brother and the home where I grew up."

As Ian replaced the tortoise his face was thoughtful. For the first time he had come face to face with someone who said quite openly that to possess something of beauty for sentiment's sake made poverty bearable. The practical side of his nature resisted this idea and for the next few minutes he sat uneasily on the edge of his chair thinking what a foolish old woman she was, not to realize her only means of capital. Leonie bridged the silence by asking if the books had come by the next train. Miss Tracy said that they had.

"But not the ones I checked off on my book list. You'll scarcely believe it, my dear, but I was sent two on economics, one on carpentry and a fourth on the breeding of rabbits for profit. How I wish I'd brought more books from my old home. My brother was a great collector."

"Perhaps the Major would let you have some, to borrow, I mean."

"I did think of asking once, Leonie, because from what Gregg tells me most of them are stacked in the attic. But, alas, the Major isn't a very approachable sort of person." She looked sorrowfully at the children. "You've already discovered that or you wouldn't have had to resort to deception to gain your own ends."

"Have we been dishonest?" asked Leonie.

"Dishonest is far too strong a word. What I mean is, I'm sad that the Major couldn't see you for what you are— three likeable children, who could bring a lot of happiness into his life."

"I expect his climbing accident soured him," said Paul.

His brother sat bolt upright.

"Who told you that?"

"Dr. Bailey."

Miss Tracy rose and hunted on a low shelf.

"I believe I still have the newspaper clipping in my

album. An old friend of mine who is a reporter sent it to me when I wrote and told him the Major had bought Mappins." The pile of gardening manuals rose high on the floor, but eventually she found what she was looking for. Placing the album on the table she invited the children to read while she went to see about lunch. "Yesterday, I couldn't have entertained you," she said, "but today I can offer you something much nicer than sandwiches."

"Goody!" exclaimed Paul. "Pretending to be sicker than you are has a beastly lot of drawbacks. Imagine! Mummy actually thought I could last on soup."

Miss Tracy laughed, and leaving them to pore over the album, went into her tiny kitchen. Ian turned over the pages. There were early photographs of Miss Tracy and her scholarly looking brother, and several more faded ones of Mappins and the gardens as they once were. Leonie would have liked to linger over them, but her brother was impatient to read the clipping. When at last he held the yellowing strip in his hand, he looked at it eagerly.

"What does it say?" asked Paul. "Did he really miss his handhold and fall with half a ton of rock on top of him?"

Ian nodded.

"Something like that. Listen to the final paragraph.

It is now learned with regret that the surgeons' fears concerning the nerve centers are correct. Major Brett Clevedon, D.S.O., will never walk again.

Ian had learned all he wanted to know, and because he felt belittled by his earlier flights of fancy, he turned on his brother.

"To think you knew all about it, when I was making such an ass of myself this morning."

"I meant to tell you, honestly I did," said Paul. "Only you were making everything sound so exciting I forgot."

"I'm as much to blame. I listened too," said his sister. "But as no one heard what you said except Paul and me, no harm's been done."

As she said this, Paul sniffed loudly. "Fish!"

Miss Tracy kicked open the door with her foot.

"Fish it is, young man." She put the dish on the table. "And I'm pretty sure you've never eaten any freshly caught from the stream before."

Ian looked at her in surprise.

"Does the Major allow you to fish?"

"Good gracious me, no. I only wish he did." Her face clouded. "I did write to ask if the privilege might be extended to me for old times' sake. . . ." Her voice trailed away.

"But you got a rude answer."

"Rude is a mild term, Ian." Miss Tracy compressed her lips as she remembered the Major's lack of courtesy. "Ah, well, it's no use piling up one grudge upon another." She chuckled. "Still, if you hear of me being locked up for poaching, don't be surprised. It isn't easy to forget the good old days. Every fourth Saturday my brother used to run a competition for the villagers. And at the end of the freshwater fishing season he presented a silver cup to the one with the biggest catch. The weights were chalked up on a slate in the village pub." She sighed. "Such fun, those days were."

Paul licked his fingers. "Who was the last person to keep the cup?"

72

"The Vicar. But no one kept the cup, only a replica in miniature." She hesitated, then went on. "Strange that you should ask because I never did discover what happened to the original. I only know it wasn't sold with the rest of my brother's sporting trophies."

"Then if you didn't catch these for yourself, how do we come to be eating a fishy lunch?" asked Ian.

"There's no mystery," replied Miss Tracy. "A few minutes before you arrived, a rather shabby-looking man brought them to me. They were a present from Gregg. So kind, so very kind of him."

6 . . . *Good Intentions Go Wrong*

Two HOURS later the children set out for Mappins. All three were preoccupied, but for different reasons. Leonie, whose arms were full of flowers from Miss Tracy's garden, was thinking about books and wondering whether she dare approach the Major. Paul, for whom the novelty of riding in a wheel chair was fast wearing off, was wondering how soon he could use his own legs. Ian was puzzling over the incident of the fish. There was no reason why Gregg should not make a present of some to the old lady, but that he should send them by the shabby, down-at-the-heels poacher whom he had scorned struck him as decidedly odd.

When they arrived at Mappins they found their father

sitting on the terrace writing notes on a sheet of paper. He looked tired but contented, and Leonie was quick to observe that a day in the open air had already given him a color. Greeting them cheerfully, Mr. Meredith asked if they had had a good day.

"Splendiferous!" cried Paul. "We met Samson, Jonah and Anthony and Cleopatra. Cleopatra isn't real and has got emeralds for eyes."

Ian hastened to throw light on this bewildering statement.

"Miss Tracy isn't nutty, although she sounds as though she might be," he added.

"An eccentric, in fact," remarked his father.

Paul was indignant.

"She isn't ecc . . . ecc . . . what you said she was. She's only a tiny bit, nicely peculiar."

"You are an ass, Paul," said his brother among general laughter. "That's exactly what Dad was implying."

"Well, it didn't sound like it to me," Paul went on stubbornly. "And I like her because she shared tomorrow's food with us." He waited while Gregg moved soft-footedly toward them, then went on in an extra loud voice. "We had fish, lovely fish from the Major's stream."

"Did you, indeed," said his father. "I had no idea the Major kept her supplied."

Gregg cleared his throat.

"He doesn't, Mr. Meredith." The words came smoothly and without any trace of embarrassment. "These kids of yours told me of a poacher they'd met on the first day here. From their description I knew it was Charlie Sparkes, a bloke what once worked here. So I says to meself, 'Up to your tricks again, are you, Sparkie boy?' And I nips down to the stream just afore you and the Major set off on your rounds."

Mr. Meredith frowned.

"And you caught him at it again?"

"More or less. I know I should 'ave nabbed him, but he's a poor, miserable specimen, and I just 'adn't the 'eart. Instead, I gives him a piece of me mind, warns 'im never to set foot on Mappins ground again, and tells 'im to take the fish to Miss Tracy. Sorry if I did wrong, sir."

Mr. Meredith shuffled his notes together.

"That's all right, Gregg. I don't suppose he's the first to indulge in a bit of poaching, but if my plans come to anything, he'll be the last."

Ian watched Gregg as he moved away. For some reason he could not understand, he felt that the explanation had come a little too glibly. But as his father appeared to be satisfied he said nothing.

"Have you really had some brainwaves, Dad?" asked Paul.

"One or two. The estate is in pretty poor shape, and so are my feet. I must have walked miles."

"Poor Daddy." Leonie ran a light finger over his forehead. "But you loved every inch of the way, didn't you? Your face looks all smoothed out."

Paul made an impatient gesture.

"All right, Paul, I'm coming back to your question. My first problem is to raise some money in order to improve the tenants' cottages and farm buildings. Here I think the stream can help."

"How?" asked Ian.

76

"Well, several people have already written to the Major asking permission to fish, and although up to now he's turned down requests, I hope I can persuade him to change his mind. I shall want your help, Lee."

"Mine!"

"Remember the unfinished masterpiece at home? Well, this time you've got exactly two days in which to design me a couple of posters for display in the village. The Duck and Dawdle would be a good place for one. Most fishy stories are told over a glass. And maybe Bassett would pin the other up in his ticket office."

"And what do I do about paints? Mine are at home."

"I know, but it's time we patronized the village shops. I'm pretty certain you'll find that the general store sells paper and poster paint. If not, try the local builder. Now it's your turn, Ian."

Ian gave a short laugh.

"Count me out. I wouldn't lift a finger to help the Major. Why should I, when he's so beastly to everyone else. You should have seen the letter he wrote us."

His father ignored the outburst.

"Very well. Then you must stop eating his food. I'm working for mine and I see no reason why you shouldn't too."

Ian opened his mouth to protest, but at a warning glance from his sister he thought better of it.

"Oh, all right, Dad," he said ungraciously. "I shall always think you're wasting your time trying to help the Major, but I'll do what you want."

"That's something anyway. You're something of a carpenter, Ian. Now I haven't had time to look at the boathouse yet. I'm told it's a bit of a shambles and hasn't been in use

since the Major came here. And the rowboat needs some repairs. See if you can make it water worthy for me before my
hatching ideas get under way."

"What has a boat got to do with chickens?" asked Paul.

"Nothing. My eggs will come from fish. I've an idea
the stream could be developed for trout fishing as well as for
coarse fishing. Also I want to do something about the conservation of supplies. It's not much use taking out if you
don't put back."

"What do you mean?" Paul asked.

"Simply that if trees are felled, new ones must be
planted. The same principle applies to a stream. That's why
I've sent for an expert to come and advise me. If he thinks
the stream suitable, we might start off with a few hundred
yearling trout."

"And how will you pay for them?" asked Ian. "I can't
see the Major opening up his money bags."

"There's the meadow and the wood. I shall harvest the
hay crop, thin out the trees and sell off the timber. Have to
get a permit, of course." As one plan after another was outlined the children's admiration for their father grew, but Ian
aired their unspoken thought.

"It's all very well making these grandiose plans, Dad.
But you've only got a month."

"What of it? A good many balls can be set rolling in that
time, and if only one or two point a way for my successor, I
shall be very well satisfied. At least they may stop the Major
worrying so much about money."

"Where is he now?" asked Paul.

"Paying his daily visit to the farm. I don't wonder you
took to that horse, son. He's old, but he's a magnificent ani-

mal. And in case you feel left out of the program, I've news for you, too."

"Shall I like it?"

"I think so. I've put things right for you with Mr. Parker, and when you're fit he says he'll find you a job or two. You always did say you'd like to work with animals."

With Paul's shouts of pleasure still ringing in his ears, Mr. Meredith went to the sitting room allotted for the family's use. The boys followed, but Leonie went to the kitchen. From the noises Gregg was making in the preparation of supper, he was plainly out of humor. Banging down a saucepan lid he eyed her sourly.

"Can't find a perishing thing since your ma's been at the spit and polish. 'Tisn't anything to laugh at, Miss. I got on well enough when the salt was in the ginger jar and the sugar in the one marked spice. Now I'm fair muddled." He pointed to the flowers. "Where did you get those from?"

"Old Miss Tracy gave them to me."

"I thought as much. Only she can grow marigolds the size of saucers. Walked off with the first prize at the local show last year." He waved a spoon at her. "The prize was one of two things—a year's subscription to a privately run library in the next town or a free joint from the butcher for six weeks. And what do you think she chooses?" Gregg snorted. "The subscription. Would you believe it? And she with hardly two pennies to rub together."

"I think I'd have done the same," said Leonie. "Have you any vases, Gregg?"

Gregg tasted the soup, made a face and again slammed down the lid.

"Never 'ad no call for vases up to now. You might find
79

a couple in the cupboard over there if your ma hasn't spirited them away."

Leonie found a glass one and a chipped blue pottery one. The flowers deserved better, but they would do, she decided. So while Gregg continued to grumble under his breath, she arranged her roses, marigolds and snapdragons. The effect pleased both her and Gregg. Picking up a tray of glass and cutlery he remarked, "Got quite a touch, ain't you, Miss. Pity the Major can't see them. Might persuade 'im to do something about the garden."

The remark gave Leonie an idea and when Gregg was safely out of the way she picked up one of the vases and carried it to the Major's sitting room. Getting no answer to her knock, she entered. The room chilled her at once—the chairs were so stiffly arranged against the walls, the cushions so primly plumped. Nor was the mahogany furniture polished, she noticed.

Saddened that a pleasant room should be so neglected, she wiped a film of dust from a low table standing in front of the window and put the vase in the center. With quick movements she arranged the chairs more invitingly, dragged the settee to the side of the wide fireplace and looked around for further improvements.

It was then that she caught sight of the shrouded picture hanging over the mantelpiece. Unable to restrain her curiosity, she lifted a corner of the cloth. To her dismay it fell into her hands, revealing a portrait of the Major in uniform. As Leonie stared she felt she had come face to face with a ghost. Then panic seized her. Somehow she had to replace the covering. But the picture hung high and she was short.

Even with the aid of a chair she doubted whether she would be able to reach the upper rim of the frame. Nevertheless she must try.

With one of the less heavy chairs dragged into position, she placed one foot on the arm and the other on the back. Then, with one hand pressed against the wall, she reached upwards. The movement caused the chair to teeter backwards and losing her balance she fell, knocking a delicate china figurine from the shelf.

At the sound of breaking china, the door linking sitting room and bedroom swung open. With an irate exclamation bursting from his lips, the Major propelled his chair into the room.

"So it's you!" he cried. "I thought at first it was Gregg moving things about. Is this how you obey my request to keep clear of these rooms?" His gaze embraced the uncovered portrait, the smashed vase and the rearranged furniture. "Is nothing safe from your inquisitive eyes and meddlesome fingers?"

Petrified with fright, Leonie could say nothing.

"Well, say something, girl. You were given a mind to think with, I suppose. Why do you imagine my furniture was arranged so? Don't you think it's difficult enough for me to get about as it is, without turning my room into an obstacle race? You're worse than your scheming brother."

"Paul isn't a schemer." Leonie found her voice at last.

"Indeed. Did you imagine that I was taken in by Dr. Bailey's wish to keep him under observation?" He laughed in a curiously mirthless fashion. "You must take me for a simpleton."

"Then if you knew, why did you let us stay?" Leonie stood in front of him holding the piece of sheeting. "Was . . . was it because you *do* like us a little bit?"

"It was not." The Major made no attempt to soften his answer. "My decision was solely one of self-interest. Mappins must be made to pay, and since your father was prepared to give me free advice and labor in exchange for board and lodging, I accepted. He's a fool, of course. His ideas are good. Given by anyone else they would have cost me a good deal of money. But he struck the bargain, not I. Once the month is up, I shall only be too glad to see the back of all of you. I hope I've made myself clear."

"Perfectly," retorted Leonie, her temper rising. "Don't worry. Not one of us will set foot in your room again. I thought I felt sorry for you, but now I don't. You're hard and at the same time full of self-pity. That's why you had your picture covered over. You couldn't bear to look at yourself as you once were. I wonder you didn't ask Gregg to hide it in the attic."

The Major's face flushed. Her words were nearer the mark than she realized. "Be quiet, child."

"I won't." Once launched Leonie could not stop herself. "Heaps of people are worse off than you. You haven't lost the use of your eyes or your arms. But you just sit and do nothing."

"Plain words from a plain little peahen."

Leonie's cheeks suddenly lost their faint color. It had cost her a lot to speak. Now she had been attacked on her most sensitive point.

"I know I'm plain and I can't pretend I don't mind. I do. But I've learned something already. I shall always have to take a little extra trouble to make something of myself."

"Quite the little philosopher," remarked the Major.

"And you think I should apply the same rule to myself. How do you suggest I should start?"

"I don't know, and I don't want to try," she said slowly, "and I'm sorry I brought you the flowers."

The Major noticed them for the first time.

"Where did they come from?"

Leonie told him.

"Stupid woman with her Mad Hatter's garden full of tortoises. If she had any sense she'd grow vegetables for the pot. You can't eat snapdragons and roses. She isn't the lady of the manor now. She's the poor church mouse chasing round for a crumb of cheese."

"At least she's a happy one," said Leonie, thinking how hateful his manner was. "And if you were anything like your portrait up there she could be even happier."

"Don't talk in riddles, child. If Miss Tracy wants to fish in the river, she must pay for the privilege. The fact that she once lived here doesn't move me in the least."

"I wasn't thinking of fishing, but of books," continued Leonie bravely. "She's old and she's lonely and very sad that she had to leave so many of them behind." She hesitated, hoping for a softening in his expression, but there was none. "It . . . it would mean so little to you and so much to her if you would allow her to come and borrow some from time to time."

"Mappins isn't a lending library," he snapped back swiftly. "She won a year's subscription, so if she wants books, she knows where to go. Do you think I don't know what's behind the request? The village is full of people with inquisitive eyes and gossiping tongues and Miss Tracy is no exception." He thumped the arm of his chair. "I am not a freak in a circus. My last penny went into this bid for peace and privacy and I intend to get full value for my money." He waved her away. "Now go, and ask Gregg to come and sweep up the results of your meddling."

"I'm going." Leonie's voice was little more than a whisper. "And I'm taking the flowers with me. They wouldn't be able to breathe if they were left in the same room with you."

Alas, for her attempt at a dignified exit. Disaster in the shape of a rucked-up corner of the rug met her as she neared the door. For the second time that evening she measured her length on the floor. Cold water splashed into her face and soaked the front of her dress. A thorn, as sharp as the Major's tongue, pierced her chin. The shock and the humiliation was more than she could bear. Struggling to her feet, she took one look at the spilled tangle of flowers, then burst into tears and fled from the room. Her father halted her as she reached the first landing.

"Lee, my dear. Whatever is the matter?"

"I . . . I . . . want to go home," she sobbed. "Please take me. I . . . I . . . wish now that I'd never answered the advertisement. He's the beastliest, cruelest man I've ever met."

Drawing her into her small bedroom, her father sat on the bed and offered his handkerchief.

"Now suppose you start from the beginning and tell me what all this is about."

Leonie wiped her eyes and told her story haltingly. At the end she added, "And that's not all, Daddy. He knows about Paul's pretend or nearly pretend illness, and no matter how good you are, or how much you help him, the Major hasn't the slightest idea of giving you the job for keeps. He's merely using you for his own ends."

"Haven't you three been doing exactly the same thing?" asked her father quietly.

"Well, yes, in a way I suppose we have, but our motives were good."

"Your behavior doesn't match up to them. Why do you suppose the Major keeps his portrait covered? Because he can't forget the past and hasn't yet learned to live with the present. By pulling off the cover you not only exposed him but brought the past and the present into collision. He's a proud man who's been humbled, a strong man made weak, and that adds up to a very unhappy person. And because he's unhappy he hits out at those nearest to him whether they deserve it or not."

Leonie nodded her head slowly.

"I said some pretty awful things. Shall I have to apologize?"

"That's for you and your conscience to decide." Her father pulled her to her feet. "Cheer up. At least you've done one good thing. You've paved the way for Paul's miraculous recovery."

7 . . . *Paul in Trouble*

PAUL LOST no time in celebrating his newly won freedom. Next morning, dressed in his cowboy outfit and carrying a clothesline borrowed from Gregg, he began twirling his make-shift lariat. An upturned pail embedded in a mound of earth was not an ideal target, but it was better than nothing. With his legs astride, he swung the looped end above his head and sent it spinning through the air. As on his five previous attempts the rope landed inches away from the target. All at once a voice behind him said, "You'd do better if you held your wrist more flexibly."

Paul swung round to see the Major watching him with a somewhat sardonic look of amusement on his face. The boy recoiled the rope.

"It's the wrong sort of rope. It's too limp. I bet you couldn't do any better."

"A good workman never blames his tools," the Major reminded him, holding out his hand.

Paul surrendered the rope and walked toward the pail. Within ten paces of it the loop fell over his shoulders, tightened and pinned his arms to his side. For a moment he stood rigid with surprise, then with a shout, he raced back to the wheel chair.

"You did it!" he exclaimed in wonder. "Where did you learn?"

"On maneuvers, with a real live cowboy," answered the Major. "Once you've mastered the knack, you never forget. Now coil the rope like this and hold the looped end so."

The demonstration was repeated again and again and some time later, as Ian and Leonie stepped out on to the terrace, they were astonished to see the Major steering his chair in a zigzag course over the long grass, and their younger brother hard behind attempting to lasso him.

"Wonders will never cease," murmured Ian. "What do you make of that?"

"A beginning." Leonie tugged at his sleeve. "Don't let them see us. It might spoil everything."

So instead of crossing the garden and following the path by the stream, they walked to the village by way of the main road. Once there, Leonie went straight to the general store where she was able to buy both paper and paint. Ian waited for her outside the Duck and Dawdle, and when she joined him, approached the landlady to make his request.

Mrs. Laudle thrust out her chest like some affronted

pigeon. Her eyes were frosty. "Indeed I will not," she declared firmly. "It's little or nothing the Major's done for any of us since he took over Mappins."

"Surely you want the village to prosper," said Ian. "I mean, if Dad does open up the stream to fishermen again, it's bound to attract trade and visitors."

"I don't deny it." Mrs. Laudle wagged a finger in his face. "All I'm saying is that no poster goes up in the private or the public saloon. Folks as live here have long memories and I, for one, won't forget how my offer of a chicken was rebuffed. Took it up myself, I did, as a neighborly gesture on the day he moved in, and had the gift thrown back in my face." Her lips came together in a thin line. "Don't come asking *me* to give him free advertisement." The door slammed.

"Looks as though you've spent money for nothing," said Ian. "Can't say I blame her. Let's see if we have any better luck with Bassett, and meet mother at the same time."

The stationmaster proved to be equally unhelpful, but not for the same reasons.

"A poster, eh! I dunno about that. Have to look up the regulations." He pulled the lobe of his ear. " 'Tis true estate agents advertise the sale of properties, but houses is one thing and fish another." As a distant whistle sounded, he brought out his watch. "That's me beauty. Dead on time. Will your ma be on it?"

Leonie said that she would. Green flag tucked under his arm, Bassett walked to the edge of the platform. Ian came up behind him.

"You're trying to say no nicely, aren't you?"

"Well, I don't want to hurt anyone's feelings, least of all your Dad's. Opening up the stream's a good idea, but it's come too late, see." His shiny, boot-button eyes were shrewd. "My guess is that the villagers have their own source of supply of fish."

"You mean from Charlie Sparkes. So they'd rather poach than pay. I might have guessed it," said Ian.

"Name me no names," said Bassett. "All I know is that if I were to pin up your poster it would be just so much confetti come the morning."

The train sidled into the station and a second or so later Mrs. Meredith stepped on to the platform. Behind her a traveling companion was endeavoring to hand out two suitcases.

"That is most kind of you," she said, signaling to her son to take them from him. The man smiled down.

"You must be Ian. Your mother's been telling me a lot about you. Where's the younger brother?"

"When last seen he was trying to lasso the Major." His mother's hand flew to her mouth.

"How awful! He really is an impossible child. Surely you could have stopped him."

"There was no reason why we should," broke in Leonie. "Strange as it may sound, the Major seemed to be enjoying it."

"Your mother tells me he is a cripple. He and the villagers must be very grateful for all your father's plans."

"I don't know that the villagers are," said Ian, disheartened by the morning's rebuffs.

A suitcase in each hand, he followed the others out of

the station. The stranger, who had by now been identified as Mr. Lester, adviser on freshwater fish conservation, accompanied them as far as the inn. Mrs. Meredith watched him disappear through the swinging doors.

"Such a pleasant man," she observed. "I've never known a journey pass so quickly."

Leonie squeezed her arm affectionately.

"It is good to have you back. Did you settle poor old Smithers into a cattery?"

Her mother shook her head. "No, I lodged him with our next-door neighbors. They seem to have taken quite a fancy to him, and he to them."

Ian rested his arms for a moment. "From the weight of these anyone would think we were to be here for six months. I hope you remembered our swimming trunks."

"I did. I also tucked in an extra trowel and small fork. If Lee's thinking of tackling the gardens, she'll need a bit of help."

Leonie looked at her mother in surprise.

"How did you know I was?"

"A hunch. Mothers do have them sometimes."

With the family reunited, lunch was a happy meal, but Paul was so full of his exploits that he almost forgot to eat.

"How long did the Major stay with you?" asked Ian.

"Not long. You see, I messed things up." Paul studied his mound of mashed potato and decided that it was an earthwork full of fossilized bones. He dug an experimental tunnel. "I told him that if he could play cowboys sitting down, he could do lots of other things as well. And that did it. He left me flat in the middle of a throw." His potato earthwork collapsed. "Then I went to see Mr. Parkes, and he said if I cleaned out the pigsties once a week, he'd let me lead the Major's horse on a rein." He wrinkled up his nose. "Pity pigs aren't coniferous animals like tigers, then they wouldn't get into such a mess. Swill is awfully swilly, you know."

His father shouted with laughter.

"Oh, Paul. If you must use such terribly long words, please, please try to use them correctly. Coniferous! That's the best yet."

"What should it have been?" Paul rescued the last of his meat cave men from the burial mound.

"Carnivorous, you clod. Tigers eat meat, not cones," answered his brother. "Don't you think he looks better, Mum?"

"Much."

"I've had a miraculous recovery. I've phoned Dr. Bailey and told him, and he says all I need now is lots of squishy chocolate cake and . . ."

"Fibber," interrupted his mother, laughing.

"Well, he did say I'd got to eat lots and lots to make up for lost opportunities and your chocolate cake is very nourishing, Mum."

"All right. I'll see what I can do. What are your plans for the afternoon?"

"Leonie's going to the attic," said Paul. "Oh, yes, you are, because before the Major got huffy, he told me that you could have all the books you wanted and do what you like with them."

Leonie could hardly believe her ears.

"He said that! Really! Oh, Paul, I could hug you."

"Just you try."

His sister, impatient for the meal to end, would willingly have gone without pudding had not her father intervened.

"First things first, Lee," he said. "Books can wait, but my posters can't. I want you to design them for me this afternoon."

"Only be a waste of time if she does," said Ian, and told of the morning's happenings.

"So that's the way of things." Mr. Meredith had clearly not expected such a rebuff. "I had no idea feelings ran so high. Pity. I shall have to go about things differently then."

"It's a shame," Lee burst out. "I've a good mind to carry sandwich boards and act as a walking advertisement just to spite them all."

"You'd never have the nerve," scoffed Ian.

"You'd be a connoisseur of everyone's eyes and you'd hate that," said Paul.

Ian groaned.

"Not again. I can't bear it. Isn't there a cure for kids like Paul?"

"Only patience," replied his father. "A connoisseur, Paul, means someone skilled to judge. The word you wanted was cynosure."

"I expect you're right," agreed his son, passing his plate up for seconds. "But as I only use long words on you, and you know what I mean, I don't think it matters very much."

"Try that logic on the eleven-plus examiners and see what happens," said Ian, scooping a bit off the returned plate onto his own.

"You beast! You've pinched all the pineapple." Paul tried to retrieve the two stolen slices, but his brother held him off until they were eaten.

Half an hour later their father departed for the wood, where he intended to select trees for felling. Paul lay on the grass busy with a jigsaw puzzle. Leonie went to the attic. Disinclined to attempt a heavy manual job so soon after lunch, Ian trailed after her.

Leonie was fascinated by attics. They held memories as well as stored bits of family history. But at Mappins the attic treasure trove consisted mainly of books. They mounted to the sloping roof. They spilled out of trunks, and littered the top of a worm-eaten table. They were slim volumes of poetry, bulky volumes of essays, children's books with moral texts and quaint illustrations, and bundle upon bundle of modern novels.

"Did you ever see such a collection?" cried Leonie. "It's bewildering. I don't know where to start. It will take days and days to sort them all out."

"Why bother?" said Ian. "Provided it's got a good story, any book from her old home will be welcomed by Miss Tracy."

Leonie squatted on her heels.

"I wasn't thinking of her alone, but of starting a lending library for the village people. The Major doesn't want the books and he's said I could do as I liked with them. The only problem is storage space. If I could solve that and lend them out at three pence a book, I'd soon have quite a lot of money."

Ian was shocked.

"You couldn't keep it. It wouldn't be yours."

"Silly. I don't want the money for myself. I want it for the gardens at Mappins. If I could only plant out the beds nearest the house, it would make such a difference."

94

Ian was tempted to remind her that she had little more than three weeks in which to put her scheme into action, but at the rapt look on her face he hadn't the heart to discourage her.

"Got to find a room first, so until you do, there's no point in sorting this stuff out. Come on, Lee. I'm almost choked with dust. Let's have a swim in the stream."

"You can if you like, but I'm not going to be caught in the reeds or get a mouthful of sticklebacks."

"You're a funk. A plain funk!" Ian was quite unable to understand her dislike of sea or freshwater bathing. "All right. I'll round up Paul. You can mount guard over our towels."

To their surprise the rug on which their younger brother had been lying was empty save for the half-finished jigsaw.

"Typical," commented Ian. "Two inches of blue sky and he gives up."

"You're a fine one to talk." Leonie marched ahead. "You took one look inside the boathouse and walked out."

"And for a very good reason. You should see it. It's got the rubbish of years stored inside. You can't even get near the boat, let alone repair it."

"Rubbish can be burned," retorted Leonie.

"Books can be sorted out." Ian grinned. "All right. Pax! We both stalled. Tomorrow we become busy beavers."

The stream came in sight, and choosing a spot where the water was deep, Ian stripped off his shorts to reveal navy-blue swimming trunks, and dived in neatly. Leonie sat on a bank among the buttercups and watched the swimmer's progress. The composition of crystal water, bobbing head and swiftly moving white arms pleased her, as did the antics of a sooty-feathered moorhen dodging in and out among the rushes.

Suddenly a loud *kree-kree* came from a kingfisher perched on a tree stump higher up the bank. Fascinated by the way he stunned his fish before throwing it up into the air and swallowing it whole, she rose and crept closer. Silent-footed though she was, the bird sensed an alien presence and, spreading its wings, skimmed low across the water to the sanctuary of a clump of reeds.

Leonie walked on further, then paused where the path curved. Twenty yards ahead, its platform foundation resting above water level on wooden piles, and its sloping roof and side wall almost completely screened by willow fronds, was the boathouse. Leonie had not seen it before, and as she stood wondering whether to venture inside or not, someone straightened himself from his crouched position at the water's edge. Seen through the shimmering curtain of dancing leaves it was hard to say whether the figure was that of a man or a boy. Thinking that it might be Paul, she called him by name. At the same instant, a shout from Ian reminded her that she held his towel. Hurrying back she found him dancing up and down to restore circulation.

"Brr!" he said, shivering. "That was the coldest swim I've had for years. Trust you to run off with my one aid to warmth." Leonie did not answer but looked expectantly over her shoulder. "I heard you shout," he went on, "but you know Paul will only come if he wants to."

"I'm not sure now that it was Paul. Poor Ian. You *are* cold. Race you back to the house."

Winning by a good yard, Ian went upstairs and returned a few minutes later with his hair plastered flat and a sweater over his shirt for extra warmth. His mother put milk and sugar into the teacups.

"No Paul yet. Lucky us," said Ian. "We can eat his share of the cake. How did Dad get on with the trees? And has he met the fishy adviser yet?"

"They're both in consultation with the Major now." All at once the sound of a scuffle broke out in the passage leading to the hall. Mrs. Meredith stiffened. "That's Paul's voice. He sounds upset."

There was a tap on the door and Gregg poked his head round.

"Could you come for a minute, Mrs. Meredith," he began. "Trouble's arrived with a capital T."

"Is Paul hurt?"

"No, my dear," answered her husband. "But if appearances are anything to go by he's in a bit of a mess." Pushing past Gregg and prodding his younger son with the tip of one finger, he ushered in the culprit. Behind him, mouth twitching, was Sergeant Bowles, the local policeman.

"Paul!" exclaimed his mother.

Paul blinked back. Egg yolk stained both his cheeks and his chin. Broken bits of shell and egg white clotted his brown hair into slimy, thick strands. Over-ripe tomatoes or what was left of them reposed like epaulets on each shoulder, from whence hung a crudely designed board bearing, in letters two inches deep, a stained invitation to fish in the Major's stream.

"*Terms moderate. Apply to the Merediths at Mappins,*"

quoted Ian, hardly able to speak for astonishment. "You mean, you actually paraded up and down the High Street wearing that!"

"Thereby causing a disturbance and a breach of the peace," said Sergeant Bowles, flicking open his notebook.

"I didn't cause anything," said Paul. "They did."

"Who's they?" demanded his brother.

Paul wiped his cheeks with the back of his hand, then screwed up his nose in disgust.

"Mrs. Laudle's beastly son, Jake, and one or two others. They didn't do anything but laugh and catcall at first, then some oaf came out of the Duck and Dawdle and gave them a bowl of rotten eggs and tomatoes." There was the beginning of a grin as he added, "I ducked and tried not to dawdle, but they were too quick for me."

"Did you recognize the one who handed out the ammunition?" asked his father.

"No, but I did hear Jake say, 'Thanks a lot, Charlie boy.' Then they let fly."

"And scored a mightly lot of bull's-eyes," remarked the sergeant. "I'll say this for your young scamp, Mr. Meredith. He's pretty nippy with his hands. Might try him as goalie in the junior soccer team. I saw him catch three eggs in a row and give as good as he got."

"Stinkers they were, too," said Paul with satisfaction. "Jake's nose got a beautiful whack. Then Sergeant Bowles had to turn up."

"And well for you I did, my lad. There was more behind it than a schoolboy lark. The ammunition might have been a bit harder when the eggs and tomatoes ran out."

98

"Are you charging him, Sergeant?" asked Mr. Meredith, searching in his pocket for silver. "I might be able to go bail for him this once."

Sergeant Bowles maintained a perfectly straight face.

"Shall we say I'm letting him off with a caution. And I mean it, lad. It's one thing to show initiative, but next time use it in a cause less likely to invite trouble. Now I'll say good night and go and give those hooligans a piece of my mind." His voice drifted away and grew faint as Gregg, a wide grin almost splitting his face from ear to ear, saw him to the door.

Paul looked round at his family.

"Haven't you anything else to say?"

"I have," said Ian. "You stink something awful."

Paul smiled the smile of someone with a job well done.

"But you heard what Sergeant Bowles said. I've got initiation, so after a bath, I think I deserve at least three slices of chocolate cake."

8 . . . Cleopatra

LEONIE SAT with the comforter bunched up around her knees writing her journal. The old grandfather clock on the landing had long since chimed eleven o'clock, but she was too keyed up to sleep. The discovery of so many books, and her half-formed plan for starting a library, filled her mind. Ian, she knew, thought the idea stupid. Yet even if she did have to leave Mappins at the end of a month, Miss Tracy, she was sure, would only be too pleased to carry on. The main problem was to find a room, and recalling her mother's recent invitation to a church social, she decided that the Vicar would be the best person to approach.

As she blew on the page to dry it, a sudden gust of wind sent the curtains billowing inwards, and feeling chilled,

Leonie tucked the journal under her pillow and snuggled down beneath the blankets. Immediately she became aware of noises. There was the voice of the stream, audible now that the wind had changed, and the high, thin cry of a small, startled animal challenged by the screech of an owl. Leonie could picture both hunter and hunted, but as she breathed a prayer for the safety of the nameless creature cowering in the tall grass, a new sound reached her—the sound of gravel crunching beneath moving wheels.

Draping the comforter around her shoulders she crossed to the open window and leaned out. The sky was a dishcloth gray, with darker clouds racing across the face of the moon as though swept by an invisible broom. All at once as her gaze fell to the terrace, the switching on of a flashlight illuminated the patch of gravel and one wheel of the invalid chair. Above this, the figure was no more than a dimly outlined shape. Hand-propelled, the small motor silent for once, chair and occupant moved slowly down the ramp and on between the ravaged flower beds until the belt of shrubs hid both from sight.

Filled with pity Leonie was tempted to dress and join the Major in his lonely night ride. Then a second thought drove out the impulse. The wheel which she had glimpsed belonged to the outdoor chair and this, she knew, was kept in the shed at the end of what had once been the vegetable garden. Moreover, to get from one chair to the other, the Major always needed the assistance of Gregg. Creeping back to bed, she puzzled over the mystery until sleep overtook her. When she woke it was morning. Hurrying over her dressing she ran downstairs to find Gregg shutting the door of the Major's sitting room.

"Good morning," she called out. "How is the Major?"

"Cross as a bear with the honey out of reach. Not that that's anything new. When he can't sleep, he growls." He waved an empty glass. "And when he's forced to take a sleeping draught, he barks. Don't know how I put up with it, really I don't."

"I do. It's because you're devoted to him." She looked again at the glass. If the Major had drunk the potion, it made nonsense of the incident in the night. Almost she began to wonder if she had been dreaming. "Are you sure he drank it?"

"Well, your flowers look healthy enough, and there ain't no sign of spilled milk on the beds outside the window." Gregg evidently thought the question odd. "Anything on your mind, Miss Lee?"

"Lots," she answered, "and top of the list is breakfast."

The family were at the cornflake stage when she joined them and talk ranged around the morning's program. Mr. Meredith and Mr. Lester had already put in two hours down by the stream, and the fishy adviser, as the children insisted on calling him, had promised to order the tanks and fish and return for their installation.

"That means I'd better get cracking on the boat," said Ian. "What about wood and seam filler?"

"Everything's been delivered," replied his father, glancing over bills for timber, pitch and nails. "But I'd rather you started clearing out the boathouse first. I'd tackle it myself, only I've got the loan of a mowing machine and while the weather holds, I want to harvest the hay."

"Dibs on helping with that," said Paul. "Lee can help with the cleaning."

102

Ian made a face.

"I bet she won't. Lee's full of some crazy idea of starting a library. You know, sixpence a week for a classic, threepence for a whodunit."

Leonie gave her brother a kick under the table.

"A library!" cried her mother. "Why, that's a wonderful idea. I'd no idea there were so many books. The Vicar will be delighted. He's already begun a house-to-house collection for unwanted novels. He wants to start a library himself and put the money earned towards a community center."

Her daughter's heart sank.

Ian had betrayed her secret, and her plan, it seemed, was not even new. Nevertheless, she was determined to cling to the second part of her resolution to bring back flowers to Mappins. Her father was the next to raise doubts.

"I know the Major said that you could do as you liked with the books, but I'm not at all sure that included the starting of a library. I think you should ask his permission first."

Leonie argued but her father stuck to his point, so as soon as breakfast was over she sought out the Major and found him being helped into his outdoor chair. Gregg had not exaggerated. His mood was black.

"What's this muck on the arm?" he was shouting as she approached. "I thought I paid you to keep these confounded things in spick and span condition. Look at it, man. Filthy!"

Gregg scratched with a fingernail and removed the offending spots. The Major glanced around. "And what do you want? Speak up, child."

"I've . . . I've come to ask you about the books," she began, wishing that her heart did not beat so fast every time they met.

"Do I have to repeat everything twice?" he snapped. "I told Paul you could do as you liked with them. Burn them. Sell them, just as long as you don't come bothering me."

"I'm sorry. It was only that . . ." Again she got no further. As the Major set the chair in motion, her attention was arrested by a glimmer of white between the spokes of the wheel. Instantly her thought went back to the night before. If the Major had not been out, how did the twisted flower head come to be caught in the wheel? Gregg's voice broke into her silent questioning.

"Got something for you in the kitchen." He returned carrying two large cans of weed killer. "Your ma said as 'ow you thought of tackling part of the gardens, so I got this stuff from the village." Screwing up his eyes he studied a label. "Selective, that's wot it says. Kills the weeds, but don't 'arm things wot should be growing." He pushed them into her arms. "That don't go for fish, mind. So take care."

Leonie promised that she would, and finding the house empty, went in search of her older brother. He was in the boathouse, half hidden by a pile of packing cases. Coils of fraying rope, anchors large and small, a rusted outboard motor and equally rusty gasoline cans littered the floor. A chipped enamel mug, a dented kettle, a misshapen frying pan and a small spirit stove stood on what had once been the workbench.

Leonie stepped over a mound of sacking and edged

her way around the tarpaulin-covered boat, slung up off the ground by means of ropes and pulleys.

"You've been a longish time," said Ian, looking up.

Leonie made no excuses but had another look around.

"What a glory hole. I shouldn't think anyone has put a foot inside for years."

"Then you'd be wrong." Ian tipped up a can and two drips of tomato soup glowed like sealing wax on the dusty floor. "You see. Freshly opened. And so is this and this." He tossed more empty food cans into a nearby wheelbarrow. "Someone's been using this place as a free lodging. And it isn't hard to guess who."

"Charlie Sparkes."

Ian nodded.

"I'll soon put an end to his little game. A stout bolt on the door and a couple of bars across the window ought to put an end to his squatter's tricks. First, we'll do a spot of spring cleaning. Lend a hand, Lee."

"If I do, will you help mix the weed killer?"

The bargain struck, the task of clearing out the rubbish began in earnest. It was hard work and not very rewarding, for even when the rubbish had been burned, much remained to be sorted out. Ian stretched his aching back.

"One look at the boat and we'll call a halt until after dinner."

With a care for rotten timber, he released the ropes and inched the boat slowly down to the ground. His sister threw back a corner of the tarpaulin, then stood silent in astonishment. Not only had the boat been recently repaired, but it had been given a new coat of varnish.

"I . . . I . . . don't understand," she said at last. "I

106

thought the boat hadn't been used since the Major came to Mappins,"

"So did I, but now I'm beginning to see daylight. There must have been some truth in what Charlie Sparks said when we first bumped into him. He and Gregg have been feathering their nests on the side. Fishing from the boat and selling the haul to hostile villagers must be highly profitable. All this rubbish strewn about the place was just so much camouflage."

"I don't believe it." Leonie pushed back her doubts. "Gregg was only too pleased when he heard we were staying. He must have known the boathouse would be cleaned out."

"Why should he? As far as I know, Dad's only spoken of his plans to the family. But suppose he did know. He'd think up some explanation. Besides we're only here for a month. Gregg's probably laughing up his sleeve, well knowing that after we've gone, everything will slip back to what it was before."

Leonie stood in the doorway where the wooden ramp sloped gently down to the water.

"I don't believe Mappins will ever be so lost again even if we do go. We shall have left so much of ourselves behind. The Major may not like us, but he won't be able to forget us."

"Rubbish! You know as well as I do that he won't give any of us a thought." He pushed his sister outside, shut the door and grasped the handle of the loaded wheelbarrow. "All the same, I'll have a bolt and padlock put on that door." He smiled mischievously. "Might get Gregg to fix them for me."

"And you'll help with the weeding?"

Ian nodded. He was still tired, but a promise was a promise. They had a sandwich lunch followed by a glass of milk, and the afternoon found them watering the overgrown paths with liquefied weed killer and tackling the flower beds with trowel and dibber. By four o'clock the mountainous pile of weeds gave proof of their industry. Ian, whose fingers were blackened and sore, was the first to give in.

"It's no good, Lee. Not another weed can I pull. If you ask me, the beds look worse than they did before we started. You'll never be able to fill in all those gaps."

Leonie's gaze wandered from the patchwork of the herbaceous borders to the stone figure of a boy crouched on a pedestal set in the middle of what had once been the iris garden. His brooding eyes seemed to confirm her brother's pessimism.

"I shall," she said, "and I'm making the first moves now by going to see the Vicar. Will you come with me?"

"Have a heart." Ian looked at her half crossly, half affectionately. "You're nothing but a female slavedriver. Do you have to do everything at express speed?"

"Yes, because time is so short."

At that moment their mother called from the terrace. With the tools and the cans of weed killer hastily dumped in the shed, both hurried indoors to wash. Later, restored by boiled eggs, bread and butter and fruit salad, Leonie was eager to start out on her second mission of the day. Wishing that he had never promised to do so, Ian went with her.

The vicarage stood in a garden adjoining the church-yard. Ivy, so thick it was like a jungle plant, climbed to the chimney pots, and the equally dark green of a cedar cast its

108

shade over the tall windows. The gloomy appearance of the house did not spread to its occupants. Pink checked and smiling, the Vicar welcomed them both.

"Come in," he cried, flinging open his study door. "Now, my dears, how can I help you?"

Slowly, but as clearly as she could, Leonie told him about the books and her plan for starting a library. His response was all that she could wish.

"I shall be only too pleased to assist. Your mother may have told you, I've had much the same idea in my own mind. One day, of course, I hope to combine it with a community center. We have a site available, but, alas, nowhere near the money required. Still, many a big project has started in a small way, and a library will bring in a useful source of income." He paused to collect more thoughts. "I think we could house it in the small vestry off the church hall. It will need a bit of alteration, but once our membership and our stock grow we can invest the profits."

Now that money had been mentioned for the second time, Leonie's nervousness increased.

"There is just one thing," she began "I . . . I . . . shall want a share of each day's takings while I'm here."

The Vicar heard her in a shocked silence. The eagerness of the girl had warmed his spirit. He shifted the notes of next Sunday's sermon.

"I'm sorry. It seems that I have misunderstood you. I thought the books were intended as a gift."

"Oh, they are," she hastened to assure him, "and I don't want the money for myself." With her words tumbling over each other she outlined her plans for the neglected gardens. "I know I shan't have nearly enough money to buy

109

rare plants, but even a few dozen geraniums and chrysanthemums would make such a difference."

"Indeed they would." The Vicar's face cleared. "I've only been to Mappins once since the Major took over, and then I didn't get beyond the terrace. Even so, my brief glimpse of the gardens saddened me. In Miss Tracy's time they were so beautiful and there was a welcome for everyone."

"And there might be again if Dad's plan comes to anything," said Ian. "At least you'll be able to fish in the stream again." He pointed to a fish in a glass case. "Was that your record catch?"

"No. Robert Tracy's." The Vicar sighed. "His sister gave it to me as a reminder of the happy, companionable hours he and I spent in friendly rivalry." As he said this, the tiny lines about his eyes crinkled upwards. "From what I hear, the proposed opening up of the fishing has already caused one member of your family to take an extra bath."

Leonie smiled back.

"You know about Paul, then."

"I do, and I very much regret the incident. In fact, I've spoken to Mrs. Laudle and she's promised that nothing of the sort will ever happen again. It proves though how strong the animosity is toward the Major."

"Will they resent the gift of books?" asked Leonie. "Need anyone know where they came from?"

"My dear child, secrets can't be kept in a village. Besides, if a library is run for profit, accounts will have to be kept."

"And you don't want me to have a share of them."

"No, I don't. When you've given the matter some

110

thought, I think you'll agree that if there are profits, someone else has a greater right to a share of them than you."

Leonie's cheeks burned. It had never occurred to her that her request would be turned down. She was hurt and angry.

"That doesn't mean you can't earn some money for Mappins," the Vicar continued. "Mrs. Laudle tells me that she is very shorthanded in the kitchen. Why not ask her for a part time job and say I sent you?"

Leonie hardly knew how she got out of the study. Dimly she heard Ian saying goodbye, but she could not bring herself to add hers. With her head held high, she did not speak until she was halfway up the hill. Then she exploded.

"How could he? It isn't fair. The books were as good as given to me, and it was my idea to present them to the library. Why do grownups always have to spoil things?"

"I hate to say it, but he's right." Ian kicked a stone into the ditch. "Morally speaking the books don't belong to the Major or you, but Miss Tracy."

"Don't you start." Leonie glared at her brother. "Miss Tracy wouldn't mind in the least, especially if she were allowed to have her books out for nothing."

"All right. If you're so sure, ask her. We're only five minutes away from her cottage."

Miss Tracy sat in the porch, a tray across her knees. Samson and Magog munched lettuce leaves at her feet.

"Hello, my dears," she called out, as Ian walked up the path toward her. "Are you enjoying an evening stroll? Such a beautiful evening. Come and sit down beside me and tell me how you're getting on at Mappins."

Ian told her about the fishing, and because his sister

111

remained silent, about the books as well. A look of pleasure lighted up the old lady's face.

"Isn't that splendid. How pleased my brother would be, especially about the books. I'm afraid I often grumbled at the money he spent. Now this heaps coals of fire on my head." She smiled at Leonie. "How clever of you to think of putting them to such a useful purpose."

Leonie did not answer at once, but stared down at the old lady's supper plate which contained nothing more than a thin slice of bread and butter, a small piece of cheese and a tomato. The frugality of the meal shocked her, for with a sudden intuitiveness she knew that this was not choice but necessity. Still she could not bring herself to say anything. Suddenly reminded of her duty as a hostess, Miss Tracy begged them to go into her sitting room while she prepared glasses of lemonade.

The children did as she asked, and as on the first occasion, Ian's gaze went straight to Cleopatra. All at once his body stiffened.

"They've been changed!" he cried.

"What are you talking about?"

"The eyes. They're nothing but worthless bits of green glass."

Leonie gazed at him in horror.

"How can you be sure?"

"By the cut and color. They look well enough from a distance, but not when you look at them closely."

His sister could still scarcely believe him.

"How absolutely dreadful," she whispered. "How could anyone be so wicked as to rob her? Poor Miss Tracy. She will be heartbroken."

112

Ian replaced the tortoise. "I hate to be the one to do it, but she'll have to be told."

Almost as he said this, she came in carrying two brimming glasses, and was at once struck by the children's expressions.

"Is anything the matter?"

Ian broke the news as gently as he could.

"Couldn't you see for yourself that the stones were different?" he added. "You'll have to telephone Sergeant Bowles at once."

To their surprise the old lady neither changed color nor seemed in any way perturbed.

"Oh dear. I thought my pitiful little secret was safe. But I didn't make allowances for sharp eyes, I see. There's been no robbery. I . . . I have been forced to sell the stones after all." A pleading look crossed her face. "I beg you to keep this to yourselves and not to ask questions."

Leonie stood over her.

"You can trust us, but I think I've guessed the truth already. It was the Major who forced you to sell, wasn't it?"

Miss Tracy said that she did not want to talk about it.

"Then Lee was right. What an absolute cad he is," burst out Ian. "And here was I just beginning to make up my mind that I'd take a job and help with her garden scheme."

"No, Ian, you must not blame the Major." The old lady's voice was firm. "He was absolutely within his rights. The cottage is his property and I've only paid a very small rent. Now, with so many plans maturing for Mappins, it's quite understandable that he needs every penny he can raise. So when he offered me the choice of buying the cottage or

113

moving on somewhere else, I had no alternative but to sell the emeralds." She looked around the shabby, cared-for room, and for the first time a tremor crept into her voice. "I'm too old to move. This is where I belong."

"Do you mind terribly, about the eyes, I mean?" asked Leonie.

"At first I did, but now the loss seems unimportant. Cleopatra is still beautiful."

"Well, I feel badly about it," continued Leonie, "be cause in a way we're responsible. If Dad hadn't had all those bright ideas for Mappins, the Major might not have pressed you. So we ought to do something to put things right. And the lovely part is that we can. When the Vicar gets the library started, he'll want a librarian. The wage won't be much until lots and lots of people join, but after we've gone, it will be lovely to think of you looking after your own books."

Miss Tracy looked from her to Ian.

"You really think the Vicar might offer me the post?"

Leonie nodded. "He as good as told me so this evening. Please say you'll take it."

"Take it? Of course I will." The old lady beamed. "It isn't the money so much, although I admit it will help. But time hangs a little heavily when one is alone. Now I shall meet people and have something useful to do once more. It's almost as if you've given a little bit of Mappins back to me."

9 . . . At the Duck and Dawdle

IAN HAD not forgotten his suspicions regarding the boathouse, yet because he liked Gregg he could not bring himself to betray him. Preoccupied with his thoughts he did not hear his father's questions. Mr. Meredith looked at his wife.

"What's the matter with offspring one and two?" he asked. "Ian seems to be up against an insoluble problem and Lee is anywhere but in the room with us eating breakfast."

Ian apologized.

"Sorry, Dad. Were you asking me something?"

"I wanted to know whether you'd give me a hand harvesting in the meadow this morning. You'll be holding a cricket match there yet if I can persuade the Major to agree. Well, what about it?"

115

"I wish I could, but I can't." Ian hated to refuse so bluntly, but his sister's cheerfully made sacrifice of the evening before had impressed him more than he would admit. And since she was determined to apply for a job with Mrs. Laudle that very morning, the least he could do was to go with her and see that everything was fair and square.

"What about you, Lee?"

"I can't either, Daddy."

"I'm willing to pay two shillings an hour for help."

"It isn't enough."

Paul's eyes grew round.

"Not enough for cutting nice clean grass, when I don't get anything for cleaning out smelly old pigsties?"

"Pipe down, Mr. Virtuous," said Ian. "You may not get paid in cash, but you take good care to be paid in kind. I saw you wolfing down a couple of pounds of apples, and they weren't windfalls either."

"Is this true, Paul? Do you filch apples from Mr. Parkes's orchard?"

"No, I don't, Dad, and Ian's a cad to say I do. Mr. Parkes said I could eat any I found on the ground. But the pigs are always there first, so you can't blame me if I help the wind a bit and shake the branches as I pass." He put out his tongue at his brother and earned a reprimand from his mother.

"Really, children. I don't know what's come over all of you this morning. You ought to be tumbling over yourselves to help your father. But as you aren't, I'll have to lend a hand myself." She waited for their protests, but none came. She tried again. "You know what that will mean. I shall get a bad dose of hay fever."

116

"Not if you tie your handkerchief into a mask," suggested her daughter. At this practical but unfooling suggestion, Mrs. Meredith gave up. All the same she was puzzled. Leonie was usually the most cooperative of her brood.

She would have been even more puzzled had she overheard the conversation between the two eldest as they made their way toward the village.

"You don't have to come with me," Leonie was saying. "I ought to be brave enough to see this through on my own."

"But you're not. I bet your heart's going a mile a minute already." Ian laughed. "What an old silly you are, Lee. The worst that Mrs. Laudle can do is to refuse."

His sensible remark was timely, for had she been alone when the Duck and Dawdle came in sight, she might well have turned and run. As it was, Ian's pressure on her elbow admitted no such escape.

"Through the hotel entrance, I think," he said.

In the small reception hall, Mrs. Laudle's son Jake was flicking a duster over a framed engraving of an early hunting scene. He was tall, big-boned and angular. One limp strand of oiled hair hung down like a comma across his forehead. Below it, his eyes were small, heavy-lidded and set too close together. From the corner of his sulky mouth a cigarette protruded. For a second or so he eyed the two in an insolent silence, then with a swagger and a jerk of his thumb over his shoulder, he said, "Round the back, you, if it's a job you're after. Ma's in the kitchen."

Ian's hand clenched to a fist, but for his sister's sake he kept his temper.

"How do you know that's what we've come about?"

"Vicar's been in." Flicking the ash to the floor he looked

117

Leonie up and down. "Shouldn't think you could do much. Wouldn't dare put you in the dining room. Customers like their waitresses to have a bit of glamor."

At his sister's sharp intake of breath, Ian saw red, but before he could redress the hurt, Leonie stepped forward. So swiftly that Jake was taken unawares, she whipped the cigarette out of his mouth and stubbed it out on his hand. With a yelp of pain Jake fell back on the red velvet-covered settee. Then, without a word, she turned on her heel and pushed her way through the swinging doors. At the entrance marked *Tradesmen* her courage seemed to desert her.

"I . . . I . . . think I'm going to be sick," she said, leaning her forehead against the wooden post.

"No, you're not." Ian thrust her head downwards. "You were wonderful, Lee."

"No, I wasn't. It was a horrible thing to do."

"Anyway, he'll think twice before he starts baiting you again."

Leonie pulled herself erect, took a few deep breaths, then declared herself ready for the next ordeal.

Mrs. Laudle was in the large, white-tiled, but none too tidy kitchen. Crates of eggs, empty bottles and sacks of potatoes and root vegetables ate up the floor space. Two bluebottles, buzzing in lively anticipation of the feast to come, circled the chopping block on which lay huge slices of stewing steak and a large dish of fish. On the hot plate of the stove an enormous saucepan of soup threatened to boil over. Mrs. Laudle lifted the lid and greeted the children through a cloud of steam. Leonie explained her visit.

"It was the Vicar's idea really. He said you were shorthanded and might give me a job."

118

"Depends," replied the landlady, "though I guess I owe you something after what happened to your younger brother." She studied the girl afresh. "Shouldn't think you had as much staying power as young Paul has." For the first time she laughed. "Spunky young scrap, he was. Because of him and because I don't hold with what my Jake did, I'm willing to meet you and the Vicar. The work will be rough, mind. No frilly aprons and pretty words to customers, but mostly doing the vegetables, washing up and helping in the bedrooms."

"I don't mind what I do," replied Leonie. "How . . . how much will you pay me?"

"Full time or part time?"

"Mornings only and not Saturdays or Sundays. You see, I must have as much time as I can spare to dig the gardens."

119

"And small thanks you'll get for it. Very well. You'll start work at eight thirty and finish at one thirty, and you'll be paid thirty shillings a week with lunches thrown in. Thirty-five without."

Leonie shut her eyes. She was not very good at sums and the figures danced in her brain. She opened them again to hear Ian turning down the offer.

"Sorry, Mrs. Laudle. It's not good enough. It's not even charwoman's pay." Pausing at the chopping block he looked down at the gleaming fish. As he did so, the swinging door leading to the passage opened, and a man appeared carrying a tray load of dirty coffee cups. To the youngsters' astonishment he was none other than the poacher, looking strangely unfamiliar in black coat and trousers. Giving the two no more than a sideways glance, Sparkes put down the tray and went out again. Ian was the first to recover.

"How long has he been working for you?"

"A week, maybe two. Why? Do you know him?" Mrs. Laudle's tone was cautious.

"Not exactly," said Ian. "We . . . we saw him once down by the Major's stretch of the stream. If you must have it, he was poaching."

The landlady laughed.

"I don't doubt it. He's a rascal, all right. Most rolling stones are. But he's a good waiter and he suits me." With her hands on her ample hips, she rocked slightly on her heels. "So you don't consider thirty shillings enough."

Ian, who appeared to be fascinated by the fish, ignored the comment.

"Jolly good-looking fish, Mrs. Laudle. From the brightness of their eyes they can't have been long out of water."
120

The landlady snatched up the dish and thrust it into her refrigerator. "Thirty-five shillings then "

"Two pounds," countered Ian, smiling his friendliest smile. "And her lunches."

At such audacity, Mrs. Laudle's mouth fell open. Then, as the boy gave another significant glance toward the refrigerator, she realized she had met her match.

"It's little short of blackmail, young man, but you played it cool, as my Jake would say. Very well. I'll agree to two pounds minus deductions for breakages." She turned to Leonie. "When can you start?"

Leonie hesitated. Mrs. Laudle looked as if she would prove a formidable employer, and the knowledge that she would have to meet Jake and Charlie Sparkes every day did nothing to allay her fears. Yet the sound of two pounds was music in her ears.

"Tomorrow," she said, making up her mind.

Mrs. Laudle nodded approvingly and turned back to the stove. At the yard door, Ian paused.

"Just one other thing, Mrs. Laudle. Will you thank Charlie Sparkes for repairing the Mappins rowboat for us. And make the most of that fish. It's the last you and your waiter will get for nothing."

As they made their way back to Mappins, Leonie worried over her brother's parting shot.

"Mrs. Laudle will never forgive you. I don't know how I can face her tomorrow."

Ian slipped the padlock he had bought from the village store into his pocket.

"Now look here, Lee. If the Major had all the money that she, Sparkes and Gregg have made between them out

121

of stolen fish, Cleopatra might still have her emerald eyes. You've simply got to stand up to people like that."

"I know." Leonie looked at her brother affectionately. "You're a wise old owl of a brother and I love you."

"Girls!" he scoffed. "Why do they always have to be so gushy?"

Leonie laughed and felt lighter of heart. It was a glorious morning. The sun climbed high and was warm on her head. Finches and tits were busy about the hedges, searching for insects and thrusting pert bills into late bramble flowers where morning dew still lingered. High overhead a lark trilled. Breaking off a spray of sweet-scented honeysuckle she thrust it into her belt.

When they reached the stream, the mowing machine stood silent in the meadow beyond and there was no sign of their father. Paul, however, was waiting for them on the stile. As usual he was untidy. But his manner was jubilant as he held out two shining half-crowns.

"I thought Mr. Virtuous gave his labor for love," teased Ian.

"You'll have to know, so it may as well be now." Paul jumped off the stile and swung around so that they had a full view of the tear in his stained and sodden shorts.

"Paul! You've been climbing trees again." His sister's voice was reproachful. "That's the second pair you've ruined in two days."

"I wouldn't be wet if I'd been climbing, silly. It was Sukie, the sow. She came up behind me when I was spreading fresh straw and ripped me from stem to stern. So I walloped her, and then I slipped backwards into her beastly feeding

122

trough. Swilly and chilly. The five shillings are workman's compensation money."

"And mark the end of your farmyard activities, I suppose," remarked his brother.

Paul allowed his sister to pin the rent together with a safety pin.

"That's what you think. Tomorrow I'm going to help groom the Major's horse, and Mr. Parkes has promised to fix up posts so that I can practice my lassoing. And from now on, my wages are to be half a crown a morning. Isn't life smashing?"

"Ripping is the word I'd use," said Ian, landing a whack at Paul's rear. He remained thoughtful for a little while and then went on: "I seem to be rather out of it. As both of you are about to earn an honest penny, I wonder if Dad would let me have charge of the yearling trout for a recompense?"

Paul stopped short.

"Leonie couldn't earn sixpence. She's much too scared of things and people."

"Jake wouldn't agree with you," said Ian, describing the morning's encounter.

His brother was impressed.

"Lee did that! Whee! Wish I'd been there. Serve him jolly well right." He ran on ahead, then stopped again as the house and gardens came into view. Below the terrace, a handkerchief tied over her nose, Mrs. Meredith was cutting the grass with a power mower. From his wheel chair the Major prodded the flower beds with a hoe.

Paul smiled a delighted smile. "We said he could do things and he can," he said, when the others caught up.

Ian took him by the arm.

"No comments, mind."

Paul jerked himself free.

"I'm not as silly as all that."

His mother brought the machine to a standstill, removed her gloves and lowered the mask. At the same time she sneezed loudly.

"There, I knew a mask wouldn't help." Another sneeze followed.

"Twice a wish," said Paul.

And another.

"Three times a letter," chanted Leonie, waiting for the fourth.

Mrs. Meredith blew her nose and suddenly became aware of her younger son's disheveled appearance.

"How on earth did you get into that state?"

"I'm worse at the back," he announced, obligingly turning around. "Sukie thought she was playing rugger. Still, I got five shillings for being made smelly again." His face broke into a disarming smile. "Lee's going to earn some money, too. She's got a job."

"A job! Whatever do you want to work for, Lee?"

"Mummy, I've just told you," continued Paul. "She wants to earn some money, though if I had to peel hundreds and hundreds of potatoes and wash up dozens and dozens of greasy plates, I'd want a jolly lot more than two pounds a week."

Mrs. Meredith put a hand to her forehead, which was already feeling heavy with the approaching hay-fever attack.

124

"Paul. Do stop. You and the sneezes are making my head reel. Is what he says true, Lee?"

Wishing her brother temporarily at the bottom of a very deep ocean, Leonie nodded.

"Yes, I start tomorrow for mornings only. Mrs. Laudle's taking me on."

Her mother looked perplexed.

"I don't understand you at all. This was supposed to be your vacation. From what you said I thought you were happy just to be at Mappins."

"Simple pleasures soon become a bore," broke in the Major. "Young people are all alike. I've no doubt Leonie hoped that her weeding efforts would be rewarded. When they weren't she wearied of welldoing and turned to potatoes and profit."

Leonie bit her lip to keep back the angry retort.

"It isn't like that at all," she said quietly, "but I'm not going to be stampeded into telling either you or Mummy why I want the money. It's my secret." With that she dashed across the grass, across the terrace and around the angle of the house.

When no one moved, Paul said, "You weren't very kind to Lee, Major. If she won't tell Mummy or me, it must be a very important secret. I expect Ian knows."

"Do you?" asked his mother.

"Yes, I do. And there's not the slightest need to worry. Lee can hold her own and isn't going to spend the money on powder and lipstick." He glared at the Major. "After what's been said, I wish she were." As Leonie had done, he, too, disappeared around the corner of the house.

"And then there were three," chanted Paul. "It's becoming a bit like the ten little Indians. Are you going to have lunch with us, Major? It's shepherd's pie and I don't mind if you have all the brown bits so long as you let me scrape out the dish."

"Thank you, but I prefer to eat on my own," the Major replied, after a momentary hesitation. Mrs. Meredith and Paul watched his slow progress up the ramp.

"Poor man," she murmured at length. "Didn't you feel it, Paul? He wanted so very much to say yes."

126

10 . . . Bolts on the Boathouse

LEONIE STOOD at the sink in Mrs. Laudle's kitchen. She had already been at work two hours and now she was patiently nicking the eyes out of her tenth potato. The mound confronting her was enormous and she wished there was someone willing to share the task. But the two waitresses who flitted in and out of the swinging doors to pour coffee and tea never so much as glanced in her direction.

The one person who did haunt the kitchen she could have done without. Civil enough when his mother was present, Jake was at his most tormenting when she was absent. Leonie judged his age to be about eighteen, and she was very conscious of his heavy-lidded gaze watching her every movement. Leaning against the drain board to her left, he puffed cigarette smoke in the direction of her stony profile.

"Not making much of a job of those, are you?" he taunted. "If you can't peel faster than that, folks will be having lunch at tea time." Another cloud of smoke enveloped her. "Course I'd give you a hand if I could. Always ready to oblige. But I had a little accident with my hand yesterday." He thrust it out so that she could see the square of adhesive tape. "Nasty thing burns. Apt to go septic. I musn't use it."

Furious with herself for trembling, but unwilling to say she was sorry, Leonie peeled on in silence. In an attempt to shut out the hard, provocative voice she thought of the garden and the flowers she would plant. Begonias would look well along the borders, and behind them the jewel colors of dahlias and the copper of chrysanthemums would combine to make a mosaic of color.

"So you prefer to play it dumb, do you?" Jake went on, glancing up sharply as the door swung inwards. "Hi, Charlie boy! Come and be introduced to Miss Chatty. Watch your step, though. She looks wishy-washy, but she's got a temper when she's roused."

Charlie Sparkes, again carrying a loaded tray, trod cat-like toward the sink. As he lowered the tray none too carefully onto the drain board, the rubbish shot from a plate into her bowl of clean water, and three cups toppled from the pile and crashed into the old-fashioned stone sink. Leonie was prepared to think it an accident until she caught the look the two exchanged.

"Now isn't that a shame," murmured Sparkes, with a wink at Jake. "Three breakages and on her very first morning too. Too bad!" Leonie swung around on her second tormentor.

"Don't you dare try to make out it was my fault,"

"Well Charlie boy didn't handle them, and as I haven't so much as laid a finger on them either, I don't know how you're going to get by Ma." Jake sidled away from the sink. "Them cups and saucers are expensive, too. Best bone china. Still, we'll let you off lightly seeing as how you're a beginner." Reaching up to a slate hanging on the wall, he chalked up, under the heading *Breakages: Three cups*—10s. "Have to do a bit of overtime to make that up, won't you?" With a final laugh at her expense the two slouched out of the kitchen.

Leonie felt too sick to think clearly. She was swamped by all her old fears of people and situations she felt were beyond her.

"I must go," she told herself. "I can't stay here another minute." She untied the strings of her apron, then paused as a round, bald head thrust itself through the open kitchen window. It belonged to a round-shouldered old man who did odd jobs about the inn.

"Don't you fret, Missy," he began. "I heard them varmints. Do 'ee stick up for your right and leave me to drop a word in the proper quarter. And do 'ee stop looking like a frightened field mouse."

As suddenly as it had appeared the head bobbed down again. The words had their effect. Wiping the slate clean, she dropped the incriminating evidence into the rubbish pail and resumed her peeling.

The morning wore on and the kitchen became hotter. Every misshapen potato, every black eye was a challenge to her inexpert knife, and eleven o'clock struck before the last one was added to the two huge saucepans. Three minutes later the sink was a lake of soapy water surrounded by mountains of dirty crockery. As she washed, dried and polished, Mrs. Laudle, who had neither forgiven nor forgotten Ian's parting shot, added her own pinpricks. Leonie was slow. Didn't she know that plates had to be rinsed before being dried? And why hadn't she taken the clean towels up to the bedrooms?

Feeling like a shuttlecock tossed hither and thither, Leonie dried her hands, put the last cups on the dresser, then picked up the pile of still-warm linen. As she was about to pass the reception desk, a man looked up from signing the visitors' book which Jake pushed toward him. It was Mr. Lester.

"Hello, Leonie," he called out genially. "I wondered if I should run into you this morning. The Vicar and I traveled down to Mapledon on the same train, and he told me he hoped you would take this job as you wanted to earn some money for the gardens at Mappins. How is it going?"

"Quite well, thank you," replied Leonie, with an uneasy glance in Jake's direction. How much had he heard, she wondered. Drawing Mr. Lester aside, she begged him to keep the reason for her job a secret. "Ian knows, but no one else in the family does. I want it to be a surprise."

Promising to say nothing, Mr. Lester asked when she was off duty. "I've got my car outside, so if you like I'll run you home after lunch. The tanks, hatching troughs and small fry are being delivered this afternoon."

All too uncomfortably aware that Jake was now straining to catch every word, Leonie hastily brought the conversa-

130

tion to a close. The rest of the morning passed in a whirl of duties, and when she sat down in the kitchen and faced her free lunch, she was almost too tired to eat. In addition, Mrs. Laudle was on the warpath.

"Now then, young lady," she began, pushing the broken pieces of china toward her. "Perhaps you'll explain these. 'Tis the pot calling the kettle black, I fancy. But I didn't hide my ill-gotten gains yesterday, as you deliberately tried to hide the results of your carelessness."

Leonie choked over a mouthful.

"I did not break the cups," she said flatly. "And if your precious son or that poacher says I did, then I'll produce my witness to prove what really did happen. And if you deduct anything from my wages, I'll go straight to Sergeant Bowles." She pushed her plate away. "Now, as I don't expect you will want me to come tomorrow, I'll take the little I have earned this morning and go."

Taken aback by this unexpectedly spirited reply, Mrs. Laudle was flustered.

"There's no call to be hasty. I never said anything about giving you the sack. I was merely going by the evidence. If someone else was responsible and I've misjudged you, then I'm sorry. I'm sure I've no wish to be unpleasant. We'll say no more about it. Now eat your food like a sensible girl." She cut a generous slice of apple tart and poured custard over it. Leonie felt her spirits revive. Thanks to the timely intervention of the old man she had been able to stick to her guns.

The landlady poured herself a cup of tea and studied her helper out of the corner of her eye.

"You're an odd child," she remarked suddenly. "Fancy taking on a tough job like this, all to put flowers in that old misery's garden." She shrugged her plump shoulders. "Don't accuse me of eavesdropping. That Mr. Lester's voice carries. What do you hope to get out of it? The Major won't fall on your neck and kiss you."

Leonie drew the apple tart toward her.

"Nothing. I . . . I . . . don't think I can explain why I want to do something for the gardens. Perhaps it's because I've got them muddled up in my mind with him. They . . . they look so crippled because no one cares for them."

"And you think when you've torn up the weeds and let in the sunshine the Major's going to have a change of heart?" Mrs. Laudle rose and refuelled the stove. "They say there's a fool born every minute. Spend the money on yourself, child. Go to the hairdresser's and have that hair of yours set properly, instead of tying it back in a brush. You've got the sort of face that can't stand being so naked. Wants framing."

Leonie thought she must be dreaming.

"Why . . . why are you suddenly so friendly toward me?"

"I dunno, and that's a fact. Maybe it's because I like the way you stood up to me. I didn't think you'd got as much spirit as would cover a sixpence." She smiled and Leonie smiled back. "Well, we live and learn. Now be off with you. And if anyone starts plaguing you again during working hours, make use of my code. One lump of sugar on the dresser and I'll give Jake a piece of my mind—two lumps and I'll know the reason why from Charlie Sparkes."

Ten minutes later Leonie was sitting beside Mr. Lester

in his car and speeding toward Mappins. Finding that the rest of the family were already at the stream, they wasted no time in joining them. Mr. Meredith and his elder son were unloading from the truck the hatching troughs, and the planking and poles painted with bitumen. Paul knelt on the ground peering into large tanks containing the small fry.

"Hundreds and hundreds of them," he shouted. "And not one of them much bigger than my middle finger. What do they have to eat, Mr. Lester?" The fishy adviser looked down into the clear, running water.

"Lots of things, including water fleas and all planktonic animals."

Paul looked up in surprise.

"I thought planktonic was a sort of friendship."

Ian shouted with laughter.

"I thought the lull was too good to last. You're thinking of platonic, you moronic misuser of the dictionary." He turned to Mr. Lester. "Isn't it a bit risky putting such small fish into the stream?"

"I agree there's a risk," he replied, "but as the Major won't hear of a properly constructed pond for a while, we'll have to do the best we can. Wire-netting roofing should keep the kingfishers and the moorhens away."

"A rearing pond will come in the future, I hope," said Mr. Meredith. "Our sort of trout farm may be a bit primitive, but at least the small fry will be in their natural element."

The stream varied in depth considerably but at last having chosen a suitable stretch, Mr. Lester, Mr. Meredith and Ian put on thigh-length waders, went into the water and began driving in the supporting poles. The sound of the hammer blows rent the air and sent every bird scattering for the protection of a small reed-fringed island.

Next the specially prepared planking was nailed on to them to form two deep troughs. Each plank had holes punched into it so that there was a continual inflow and outflow of water. By five o'clock the netting roof was in position and the small fry scooped up in nets and introduced to their new home. Paul lay on his stomach and watched. Beneath the surface, close-ranked as an army, the brown babies darted this way and that.

"Dibs on giving them their first feed," he said.

"That's my job," said his brother. "You stick to your pigs and your horse."

Mr. Lester gave instructions.

"Let them scavenge for themselves most of the day," he began, "but for the evening feed you must give them cooked beef liver or heart, so finely minced that it looks almost milky on the water. Later on, they'll need a midday meal as well, and for a change you can give them cod roe, hard-boiled egg and cracker meal." He smiled. "Quite a diet. Don't worry. I'll leave you the full menu and quantities before I go."

There remained only the hatching troughs to store. Like the wooden planks sunk into the bed of the stream these were also painted with bitumen, but they were fitted with shallow trays to hold the eggs. Suggesting that the boathouse might be the best place, Mr. Meredith and Ian carried one, and Mr. Lester and Paul the other. Paul was curious.

"How do the eggs get into the trays?"

Mr. Lester explained that it could not be left to nature

134

because so many eggs would be lost, and that the trout farmer had to express them by hand and fertilize them by adding a small amount of milt from the male.

"How many eggs does a female lay?" asked Paul.

"At a guess, something like eight hundred eggs for each pound weight, so you see, Paul, with each trough holding two hundred and fifty thousand eggs this stream could become a gold mine to the Major. Still, hatching is some way off yet, but when their spawning season does come round, I think you'd better send for me again."

"You bet we will." Paul's enthusiastic expression changed. "I forgot. We shan't be here. It will be Dad's accessory who will send for you."

"Successor," corrected his father with his customary patience. Putting down the trough he waited while Ian unlocked the boathouse. Inside, he looked about him with pleasure.

"Nice work, son. The place certainly looks a lot tidier than when I first peeped in through the window. Tomorrow, perhaps, you could have a go at the boat. I've almost persuaded the Major to join me for a bit of coarse fishing further downstream. Getting him into the boat shouldn't be too difficult with Gregg lending a hand."

Ian whipped off the tarpaulin and lowered the boat. His father ran a hand along a varnished seam.

"As sound a bit of carpentry as anyone could wish. Congratulations again. When did you manage to fit in the repairs?"

"I didn't." Ian unraveled a rope. "I've been meaning to tell you for days. The boat was already repaired when Lee and I began tidying up. Someone had been using the boat-house as a freelodging and the boat for poaching operations. That's why I fixed bars across the window and bought a padlock for the door."

"And you have a shrewd idea who that someone was."

"I think so, Dad." Ian hesitated. "But as I've no proof, I'd rather not mention names."

Mr. Lester nodded.

"Wise boy. All the same be warned by me. If the poacher's a countryman out for the odd fish you can afford to turn a blind eye. But the chap who makes a living at the game is a different customer altogether. One poacher I knew used dynamite and ruined the fishing for years. Shock waves killed them off in hundreds."

That evening they acted on Mr. Lester's advice, and renewed the *Fishing Prohibited* notices at intervals along the whole stretch of the stream. Ian did not place much faith in them, but he went to bed tired and satisfied with the day's work. For the first time since coming to Mappins his imagination had been awakened, and the knowledge that he had been made custodian of the stream filled him with pride and pleasure.

The days that followed were busy. Leonie began to enjoy her mornings at the Duck and Dawdle, and to her surprise neither Jake nor Sparkes tormented her again. She did not forget Mrs. Laudle's advice about her appearance, either, and while she did not go to a hairdresser's, she did persuade her mother to cut her hair to shoulder length. By dampening it and pinning it into curls each evening, she found that it had a natural tendency to wave. No one was more delighted than her mother.

136

"Much softer," she commented. "Pony tails always did strike me as being a lazy form of hairstyle. Dare I ask what brought about the change?"

Ian grinned. "She's got a crush on Jake, though what she can see in that pasty-faced hood beats me."

Leonie pummeled him with both fists and tugged his hair.

"Take that back," she demanded, giving the tuft a twist. "Go on. At once."

"All right. If it isn't Jake, then you must have a case on Charlie Sparkes."

"Oh, how could you?" She pushed him away from her in disgust. "I don't even look at him, let alone speak to him."

"That will do, you two," said their mother. "Whatever the reason, I like the change. It's a great improvement."

Leonie made a face at her brother, then went out to her weeding. On another afternoon she began sorting out the books the Vicar had promised to collect as soon as the vestry was ready to receive them. Ian had promised to help her, but more and more of his time was devoted to the care of the baby trout and the cultivation of a bed of watercress. Both tasks he found absorbingly interesting and pointing a way to his future. Even if he had to leave Mappins, there were several other trout farmers in the country who might be willing to give him a job. Only Gregg seemed to be depressed.

"Who's to carry on when you're gone, that's wot I'd like to know," he grumbled one evening, as Ian forked a lump of liver out of a saucepan. "You won't catch me mincing up that stinking muck."

"Full of vitamins though." Ian fed it to the meat grinder. "What's up with you these days, Gregg? You used not to be so gloomy."

"Can't always be a perishing ray of sunshine," he answered. "I tell you straight. I'm not taking on any more jobs."

"Nobody's asking you to," said Ian. "What's to prevent the Major taking over? He could, you know. Be a sort of hobby for him."

Gregg snorted, and muttering something that sounded like "and fish might fly," he stumped out of the kitchen. As he did so, Mrs. Meredith came in and began rummaging among the shelves in the larder.

"That's odd," she murmured. "Paul's demanding soup, and I can't find the can. I know I ordered a large-sized one."

"Perhaps Gregg's been having a midnight feast, or you've forgotten you've used it," said Ian, scooping the last of the mince into his long-handled fishing net.

"Don't be silly, darling. The groceries were only delivered yesterday, and we had steak-and-kidney pudding for supper." She took the key to the boathouse from the hook. "Before I forget it. Lee wants this. Miss Tracy's given her some late-flowering carnations in pots and she wants to keep them in the boathouse until she's decided where to plant them."

Ian took the key and hurried down to the stream. The sun was setting over the tall line of poplars and gilding the surface of the water with paillettes of gold. His sister joined him, carrying the two half-empty cans of weed killer. Ian eyed them apprehensively.

"Mind how you go with those."

Sitting at a safe distance, she watched while the fish were fed. The minced liver floated to the top and a second later the surface was a threshing mass of gaping mouths and speckled brown bodies.

138

"No need to summon them to the cookhouse door," said Ian. "They're the hungriest little beggars I've ever come across."

The antics of the tiny fish were entrancing, but with their own supper no more than half an hour away, the two hurried to the boathouse. Miss Tracy's gifts were already lined up outside the door and Leonie lost no time in arranging them on the workbench below the window. Suddenly, as she stepped to one side, her foot rattled against something. Ian stooped and picked it up. It was the empty soup can.

"So this is where the beginning half of Paul's supper got to!" he exclaimed.

"What do you mean?"

Ian explained about his mother's search.

Leonie tucked a slender stick in to support one of the stems.

"That's very peculiar."

"Horribly so," agreed her brother, "because if this is mother's missing can then someone stole it and made use of the boathouse again."

"How could they, when the door was locked?"

"Exactly. Don't you see, Lee? Only one person outside the family knows where the key is hung, and that person is Gregg."

11 . . . *Niche in the Chimney*

LEONIE AND Ian discussed the matter again after Paul had
gone to bed.

"Perhaps that's why Gregg's been so short-tempered
lately," said Ian. "He's seen the trout farm as a threat to his
poaching activities."

"It doesn't ring true, somehow." Leonie drew the bedroom curtains together and began pinning up her hair. "He
isn't sly like Charlie Sparkes. He's straightforward and
decent."

"Then how do you explain these?" Her brother drew
from his pocket an envelope containing two or three coarse
threads of natural-colored tweed. "I didn't show them to you
before, but I found them on a nail near the boathouse door.

140

Someone caught the sleeve of a jacket on it, so when we've traced that we've got our man."

Leonie yawned sleepily.

"I can't argue about it any more. The most sensible thing would be to tell Daddy or Sergeant Bowles."

"I might at that. A police watch on the stream wouldn't be a bad thing."

As soon as Ian had gone, Leonie undressed and got into bed. Yet tired though she was, sleep was a long time in coming. When it did, she dreamed that she was surrounded by jackets, all in a different state of disrepair. It seemed terribly urgent that they should be mended, but every time she threaded the needle, the strand was never longer than the ones Ian had shown her.

A cold drip on her forehead woke her. It came from a sponge held high above her head.

"At last," said Paul. "I thought you were never going to wake up. I've been aiming at your left eyebrow for the past ten minutes, but you do wriggle so when you're asleep."

Leonie struggled to a sitting position.

"Honestly, Paul. You do the stupidest things. You've soaked my pillow. What time is it?"

"Half past nine and a fine Saturday morning. Mummy said you were to sleep on because you and Ian were so late going to bed last night." He frowned. "You shouldn't have been late. You came up soon after I did. Were you telling secrets?"

"Of course not."

"Fibber. I know you were, because I crept down and listened outside your door."

"How much did you hear?"

"About Gregg and the coat." He gave her a sly glance. "I know the answer to that, I mean, who the coat belongs to." He squeezed the last drop of water onto his palm and licked it.

"Who?"

"You have secrets, so why shouldn't I?"

Leonie resorted to coaxing. "Come on, Paul. You know you want to tell."

"Will you do something for me if I do? It isn't anything horrid. I only want you to let me lasso you. A post is all right, but if I'm to become an expert I need a moving target."

"All right," she agreed, thankful to be let off so lightly. "Now what's your secret bit of information?"

"You've got to earn it first. You might decide only to be a target for five minutes. I want you for at least half an hour."

Leonie slid her toes out of bed.

"You're the most maddening brother any sister could have. If I do do it, you'd better be good. That rope of yours stings."

Pushing him out of the room she rejoiced all over again that it was Saturday and her free morning. Yesterday's dress hung over a chair. Discarding it in favor of a green and white spotted one she dressed, and brushed her hair until it fell loosely about her face. Sunshine and fresh air had restored the glints, and the softer style certainly did give an added roundness to her cheeks. Pleased with what she saw in the mirror she ran downstairs to begin the day.

The dining room was empty and all traces of breakfast had been cleared away. In the kitchen Gregg was polishing silver. The sleeve of his shabby jacket fell back from his wrist, and as he held the silver candelabra up to the light and rested the other hand on the table, Leonie drew in her breath sharply. Below the elbow was a jagged, three-corner tear. Observing her look of dismay, Gregg said, "Anything the matter, Miss Lee?"

"Nothing," she replied quickly. "I was looking at your sleeve. Did you know you'd torn it?"

"Yes. It's only an old coat me and the Major take turns in wearing when we're doing dirty jobs."

"When did it happen?"

Gregg shook the can of polish.

"Does it matter?" His eyes narrowed. "You're acting peculiar-like."

"No, I'm not." Leonie plucked up her courage. "I expect you tore it when you went into the boathouse. Ian found some strands caught on a nail."

"Did he indeed." Gregg's voice was sarcastic. "And what's that meant to prove? As a matter of fact I haven't been near the boathouse since it became all exclusive with a bolt and padlock."

"Well, a tear doesn't just happen."

"Are you giving me the third degree?" Gregg was fast losing patience. "Maybe I took a pair of scissors and cut it myself. Maybe the Major tore it last time he went to visit his horse. How should I know? I've got work to do, and if you're wondering where the rest of your family is—your ma's gone shopping, your father and Paul are at the tree felling and Ian said I was to tell you that the Vicar would be here at eleven to collect the books."

Leonie said no more. With a slice of bread and butter in one hand and an apple in the other she went out onto the terrace. The morning sparkled. Dew glistened on the grass. Birds chirped from the bushes, sunlight warmed the old walls of the house and a whispering breeze sent the poplars swaying like stately dancers. Her simple breakfast eaten, she climbed to the attic and found Ian already parceling the books.

"The coat proves nothing," she informed him. "It could just as easily have been torn when the Major was wearing it."

"I know." Ian drew another pile of books toward him. "I tackled Gregg about it after breakfast."

"Oh dear," said Leonie. "So did I. No wonder he was angry."

For the next hour or so they worked in a companionable silence, and when at eleven promptly the Vicar's car rumbled up the drive, the last of the books had been carried down to the hall.

"My word!" he exclaimed, appearing in the doorway. "I had no idea there were so many. I hope my back axle will stand the strain."

Armful by armful the books were loaded into the car and at last they set out for the village.

"Will Miss Tracy be there?" asked Leonie, sitting on her brother's knee in the front of the car.

The Vicar said that she would.

"She's never ceased talking about the library and the job you've given her. It was a generous act, my dear."

"I couldn't do anything else after what you said. And I'm glad now. Working for my flower money is hard, but it's more satisfying than simply taking it out of library funds."

"I hoped you would think so." The Vicar slowed up to allow a straggle of cows to pass. "How is your fund getting on, by the way?"

"Not badly. I've got nearly five pounds so far; at least Mrs. Laudle's minding it for me. I did a bit of overtime last week."

A few minutes later the church spire loomed up among the trees. Bringing the car to a standstill beside the grass border, the Vicar took a bunch of keys from his pocket and unlocked the church hall. The vestry adjoining it was larger than Leonie had imagined. In one corner was a pile of planks, and opposite was a bench fitted with tools. Ian was pleased.

"I see you've got everything laid out."

"Everything except skill. I'm hoping you can supply that."

"I have done a bit of carpentry at school."

"Good." The Vicar took off his jacket and rolled up his sleeves. "Then this is where I play the apprentice to your great experience."

The task was begun with enthusiasm. Leonie was not idle either and by the time Miss Tracy arrived, she had already sorted out many of the books.

"Good morning, Vicar. Good morning, my dears," she began. "I see you've made a brave start." Placing a sheet of newspaper on the floor and pinning her long skirt up above the petticoat to shield it from dust, she knelt beside Leonie and picked up first one and then another of the children's books. "Dear me! What memories these bring back. My father, I remember, gave me *The Water Babies* on my eighth

145

birthday. The story fascinated me. Every night I used to peer up the chimney hoping to see a small sweep. My only rewards were a shower of soot and one small bird's nest that fell down and lodged itself in a niche. My brother was delighted with that. He used to hide things in it when he was pretending to be a Royalist hiding valuable documents from the pursuing Roundheads. That niche was the nearest thing to a genuine secret hiding place we had at Mappins. Who knows? Some of his treasures may still be hidden there."

Leonie enjoyed listening to stories of Miss Tracy's childhood, but quite suddenly the old lady turned to more practical matters. When the time came for lunch, which was eaten picnic-fashion in the Vicar's study, she had printed subject headings on slips of paper and stuck them on the first shelves Ian had erected. Lunch over, she was the first to resume work, and was so unsparing of her energy that by four o'clock the last of the books were in place.

"Of course we ought to have painted the shelves," she remarked, patting the books into line, "but trimmings can come later. What we need now is a rubber stamp and a cash box. Then we can open."

"We ought to have a proper ceremonial opening," declared Ian. "What a pity we can't persuade the Major to officiate."

"Ceremonial openings can wait until we get our community center," said the Vicar. "By that time the Major may well be the one to turn the silver key." The Vicar locked the door behind him.

When he had taken the old lady home, the Vicar turned his car in the direction of Mappins.

146

"A remarkable woman," he observed. "Many would have been soured by the loss of such a beautiful home. But not Miss Tracy. Fortunately, nothing can ever destroy her happy memories."

At once Leonie was reminded of *The Water Babies* and the niche in the chimney. What fun it would be, she thought, if it did still hold relics of a lost boyhood. Determined to look as soon as she could, she added her thanks for the lift home, then tugged her brother toward the Major's sitting room. Paul, however, barred her way.

"You promised," he began, uncoiling the rope tied around his middle.

"Bother!"

"What's he getting at?" asked Ian.

"We struck a bargain. I was to be lassoed in exchange for secret information about the coat." Her face brightened. "But I know it already. Gregg told me it belonged to the Major."

Paul's mouth drooped, then, as quickly, his face brightened.

"But you didn't know when you promised, so you can't wriggle out of it."

He dragged her back to the garden. Leonie did not enjoy the next half-hour. It was one thing to run for the sheer joy of movement but quite another to be pursued by a whooping young fiend armed with a spinning rope. It lashed at her shoulders; it bit at her ankles. But the more Ian jeered the more determined Paul became. At last, when the half-hour was almost up, he tasted success. As Leonie stumbled and panted along by one of the weeded flower beds the rope fell accurately, and in the next instant her arms were pinioned. Paul yelled his triumph.

"I've done it. I've done it at last!"

"And about time too." Leonie sank to the ground exhausted. "I'm out of breath and I ache all over."

Paul released her and coiled his rope.

"Now you can tell me your new secret. Why did you want to go to the Major's sitting room?"

"He doesn't miss a thing, does he?" said Leonie. "I wanted to put something Miss Tracy said to the test."

Ian ridiculed the idea.

"Honestly, Lee. You get sillier and sillier. As if anything could be hidden in the niche after all these years."

"Treasure!" exclaimed Paul. "Whoops! I'm with you. The Major's still in the wood with Dad. Come on. Let's look now."

The Major's room was as cold and as impersonal as it had been when Leonie first entered it. The cotton shroud still hid the portrait, and there were no flowers in the vase. Kneeling before the hearth she put her hand up the chimney. A thin spattering of soot cascaded down to the empty hearth, then, as she groped first to the left and then to the right, her hand closed on something smooth and cold. She withdrew it and there was a gasp from Ian.

"The silver cup!" he cried. "We've found the fishing trophy."

"That thing," said Paul, in disgust. "It's as black as night. How do you know it's the cup?"

"Couldn't be anything else," answered his brother. "A soaking in hot soap suds and a bit of polish and we'll soon

148

have it shining as good as new. Wonder why the old boy hid it in the chimney?"

"Perhaps because he didn't want it to be sold with the other things," said Leonie. "He must have known that was what would happen. Poor Robert Tracy." She turned to see her younger brother's head almost lost to sight up the chimney. "Paul, don't. There's nothing else there."

Her words were too late. As she and Ian leaned forward to tug him down, there was a heavy enveloping fall of soot. Paul collapsed on top of them choking and spluttering. Ian held him off as best he could, then groped for his handkerchief. Leonie was almost in tears. Face, hair and hands, as well as the front of her dress, were covered with greasy soot.

"I'm filthy," she wailed. "Absolutely filthy. And it's all your fault, Paul."

Ian spat on his handkerchief and wiped his face, leaving zebra patterns from eyes to chin. Paul choked again, tested his eyes and found that he could still open them. The surrounding dirt made them intensely brown.

"I've remembered something," he remarked suddenly. "Gregg's let the boiler out, so the bath water will be cold."

12 . . . *Weed Killer*

"To THINK that we're more than halfway through our stay here," remarked Mrs. Meredith at breakfast on Monday morning. "It doesn't seem possible that by a week from Saturday I shall be doing the weekend baking in my own kitchen."

Breakfast had been a far from talkative meal and this unfortunate observation deepened rather than relieved the gloom.

Paul put his hands over his ears.

"Don't. Why do you have to make it sound so horribly near?" He began counting off the days. "Eleven more. How many hours is that?"

"Oh, work it out for yourself," said his brother.

"Anyway, it's thousands and thousands of minutes," Paul went on, visibly cheering up.

"And you can spend thirty of them digging for bait," added his father. "As soon as I've done the round of the cottages collecting the rents, I'm going to try my own luck with a rod and line."

Paul dipped his bread into his brown egg. The yolk, he decided, was a volcano that might erupt at any minute, but despite his fancy he still had an ear for business.

"How much is a full can worth to you? A shilling?"

"We'll decide that when you've filled it. And remember. I'm not to be taken in by an under layer of snails. I want worms and nothing but worms." Mr. Meredith folded his napkin and rose from the table. "By the way, Lee. The Major wants a word with you."

Immediately she was panic stricken.

"Why me? Why not the others?" Her gaze flew to the blackened trophy standing on the sideboard. "We were all in disgrace together. Besides, I can't possibly see him now. I'm late as it is, and Mrs. Laudle can't bear unpunctuality."

"I'm sorry, my dear, but you'll just have to explain. I'm sure Mrs. Laudle will forgive you for once. And don't look so scared. The Major isn't an ogre. All of you were in the wrong on Saturday, but he agreed with me that soot, a tepid bath and a scrubbing down with cleanser was punishment enough. So if you're fearing a scolding on that score, forget it."

His daughter was far from being comforted. If what her father said was true, there could be only one other reason for the summons. The Major had heard about the library and was angry. There was no escape, however. Two minutes later, her heart fluttering like a caged bird, she knocked on his door. The Major sat by the open window reading a letter.

"Good morning, Major," she began. "Daddy said you wanted to see me. Is . . . is it about the library?"

"So your conscience is troubling you," he replied, without looking up. "I'd begun to wonder if you had one. When I said you could have the books I was thinking of your own amusement, not that you should turn them into a money-making proposition. You've taken advantage of me."

Leonie kept her eyes fixed on a tiny cloud floating high in the blue.

"I didn't mean to. I tried to explain my plan the morning you were so cross about the stains on your chair, but you wouldn't listen. And you did say that I could do as I liked with them."

"I did. I admit it, so I withdraw my last remark." He flicked the letter with his thumb. "All the same I want no more letters like this. I am not a public benefactor and I have no wish to pose as one. You will kindly make that clear to the Vicar when next you see him." Leonie sighed with relief. She had been so afraid he would demand the return of the books. "There's another thing," he went on. "I promised your father I wouldn't dwell on Saturday evening's unfortunate escapade, but I confess myself curious to know what prompted the search of my chimney."

Leonie swallowed with difficulty.

"It . . . it was because of something Miss Tracy told me when we were sorting out the books. Her brother used to hide things there as a boy, so I thought I'd have a look and
152

see if anything remained. That's how I found the silver cup. I . . . I . . . do so wish it could become a fishing prize again."

The Major flung down the letter and said with some annoyance, "That will do, child. Your mind hatches too many plots. You're a scheming little minx." His lips twisted as if in pain. "Now be off with you, and have the goodness to ask Gregg to come and give me a massage."

Leonie did as he asked.

"Do the Major's legs often trouble him?"

Gregg washed his hands at the sink.

"Frequently. You might call them a sort of barometer. All quiet from the knees downwards and the wind's from the south. If not, look out for squalls." He reached for a towel. "Have to give your father the know-how when I go off for a couple of days."

"You're going away!"

His manner changed abruptly.

"I can 'ave a bit of time off, can't I? If anyone's earned it, I 'ave."

"Of course. But why sound so miserable?" Leonie's voice softened. "I've a feeling something's wrong and that you're worried."

"And you're right." He shook his head sorrowfully. "Why you kids couldn't keep the soot to yourselves instead of shaking yourselves like puppies, I'll never know. Hours it'll take me to get that rug clean."

"Gregg, I'm sorry, truly I am. Look, I'll tell you what. Leave it for me, I'll shampoo it when I get back." She glanced at the wall clock. "Now I must fly. I'm half an hour late as it is."

Fortunately Mrs. Laudle accepted her explanation.

153

"And now misery wants the books back, I suppose," she commented.

Leonie shredded a runner bean.

"No, he called me a scheming minx, but somehow he didn't sound horrid like he usually does, but rather as if he were secretly pleased."

The morning slipped into its customary rhythm. Jake slouched in and out of the kitchen, the inevitable cigarette drooping from the corner of his mouth. Sparkes worked in the store room and gave the kitchen a wide berth. By three o'clock, having stayed an hour later in order to make up for her delayed start, Leonie decided to call in at the vestry library. The afternoon session had not yet begun and a small knot of people stood waiting outside for Miss Tracy to arrive. Leonie stood shyly apart, but could not help overhearing what was being said.

"If you ask me, 'tis a judgment," declared a stout woman, whom she recognized as Mrs. Dawson, the butcher's wife. " 'Tis he who turned his back on us. I don't hold with it, but if someone's getting his own back, the Major's only himself to blame. And so I shall tell Sergeant Bowles if he comes asking questions."

"He'll do that all right, me dear," said another. "He be like one of Miss Tracy's tortoises, slow but sure. And 'tis a police matter I'll be bound and not carelessness on the part of any of them young folk."

The butcher's wife shook with laughter.

"Perhaps Sergeant Bowles will come round to the idea that one of us did the deed. We've all of us bought the stuff at some time or another." She poked her neighbor in the ribs.

154

"And not one of us but hasn't taken the frying pan to a nice fat bream or two." Her voice became more subdued as she caught sight of Leonie for the first time. "Joking apart, 'twas a dirty trick and a poor return for all the good work those Meredith folk have put in."

Leonie could listen no longer. She went up to the group.

"Please, Mrs. Dawson, I couldn't help hearing what you said," she began. "Is anything wrong at Mappins?"

Mrs. Dawson shifted her shopping basket and balanced it on her hip.

"Do you mean to say you don't know? Where have you been all the morning?"

"Working for Mrs. Laudle at the Duck and Dawdle. Please tell me."

Mrs. Dawson looked uncomfortable.

"Don't know as I should, though you may as well hear it from me as from anyone. It's the trout farm your father started. It's been wiped out. Your brother made the discovery when he went to give the fish their midday meal. Seems he and your father sent for Sergeant Bowles."

"Wiped out!" Leonie stared at her in bewilderment. "You . . . you mean the fish are dead? It isn't possible. One or two, perhaps, but not all of them."

"To the last little tiddler."

Leonie did not wait to hear more, but ran and ran until loss of breath forced her to a walking pace. It couldn't be true, she told herself. Yet when, panting and hot, she reached the familiar stretch of water and saw the group standing on the bank, she knew that it was. She ran the last few yards.

155

Her father's face was grave. Ian was white. Paul was openly crying. Leonie forced herself to look into the water at the hundreds and hundreds of floating bodies. Then she clutched her father's arm.

"They told me about it in the village. What happened, Daddy? They were prefectly all right yesterday."

Sergeant Bowles, who had been examining the ground, straightened himself and came toward them. In his hand was a fold of blue paper containing some whitish-gray powder.

"Think perhaps you might be able to help us there, Miss. See this powder I've scraped up from the bank. Can you give it a name?"

Leonie had used it too recently not to be able to recognize the smell and the texture. Her face rigid with dismay, she said, "It's weed killer."

"Ah!" Something like a sigh escaped from the policeman's lips. Then silence reigned. Leonie looked from one face to another.

"Why are you all staring at me? You . . . you couldn't possibly think I did it."

"Not intentionally, Miss." Sergeant Bowles's voice was clipped and precise.

"Let me put it to her," broke in Mr. Meredith. "Stop shivering, Lee, and think quietly before answering my question. Have you on any occasion left the cans of weed killer lying about?"

"Never. I'm sure of it."

"What about the evening we put Miss Tracy's carnations in the boathouse?" said Ian. "You had the cans with you then. I remember warning you to be careful. What did you do with them afterwards?"

156

"I . . . I'm . . . almost certain I left them in the boat-house." Her forehead puckered up in the effort of remembering.

"It's no good being almost sure," Ian said again. "You could have left them on the bank."

"I didn't. I didn't." Leonie almost sobbed out her denial. "Tell him you believe me, Daddy."

"I want to, Lee, but you see the cans aren't there. We've looked."

"They could have fallen down and rolled under the bench," she suggested.

"No use, my dear. We searched thoroughly."

"Then they were stolen. That's it," she went on, more confidently, "they were taken by the same person who's been using the boathouse as a free lodging."

"That won't do either," said Ian, "because ever since we found the empty soup can, I've kept the key in my pocket. It's never left me." He kicked miserably at a stone.

157

"I see." His sister began shivering again. "Well, why doesn't one of you say what you're all thinking—that I did forget the cans and that they rolled down the bank into the water and poisoned the fish?" No one answered her, and with a last desperate look around, she turned and fled from the scene. Mr. Meredith would have followed her, but Sergeant Bowles held him back.

"Best not, sir. Either way she's had a bit of a shock. Leave her to herself a bit." He took out a handkerchief and wiped his forehead. "I'm right sorry it had to end like this, Mr. Meredith. But the evidence being what it is, you can rule out the idea of foul play."

"Can we?" With his legs wide apart and his cheeks still bearing the tell-tale signs of grief, Paul twiddled the end of his lariat. "Lee's an awful silly sometimes, but she doesn't leave things about, not important things like cans of weed killer."

"And where does that get us, sonny?"

"Quite a long way," answered Paul, "because, you see, if Lee had forgotten and the cans had rolled down the bank into the water, they'd still be in the shallows, wouldn't they? But they're not, 'cause while you were talking I looked."

Sergeant Bowles flung himself down on the bank and so did Ian. Together they pushed back the clumps of buttercups and the tangle of seeding grasses and together they explored the underwater sides of the bank.

"He's right," said Ian. "Not so much as a label to be seen. Where do we go from here, Sergeant Bowles?"

158

13 . . . The Moorhen's Nest

"FOR GOODNESS' sake, stop acting like a leaky tap," said Ian. "You look horrible with your nose and eyes all red from crying. You've had a whole night to realize that, thanks to Paul, you're in the clear."

"Am I?"

There was no confidence in Leonie's voice. She felt sick at heart and could not readily dismiss the unspoken accusations. Nor could she forget the scene she had witnessed. It was as if autumn had come suddenly to the stream, the dead fish floating on the surface like hundreds and hundreds of withered, brown leaves. "You're only saying that to comfort me," she went on. "Daddy's walking about like a thundercloud. Gregg won't look me in the eye, and when I passed the Major's door just now his voice was as cold as when I accidentally uncovered his portrait."

Ian made an impatient gesture.

"Oh, heavens! Why do you have to act the tragedy queen and dramatize everything so? Of course Dad and the Major are angry. So am I. It's a horrible end to a brave project. Those . . . those little fish were so alive. I think they were beginning to know me. Oh well. What's the use. I think I'll go and ask Parkes if he can find me a job."

Left to herself, Leonie looked in the mirror and decided that her brother was right. She did look terrible. Fortunately for her, the wind and the sunshine were helpful, so that by the time she reported to the inn for work, the blotchiness had gone from her skin. Nevertheless the girl's subdued manner did not escape the astute eyes of the landlady. Being a blunt and forthright woman, she wasted no time on sympathy.

"Work's the best remedy for you, my dear," she began, hovering like a genie over her saucepan of stewing bones. "Nothing like it for taking the mind off things."

"You've heard what happened then," said Leonie, tying her apron strings.

"Bless you, you can't keep news from traveling in a village this size."

"And are people still saying that it's a judgment on the Major?"

"Not since the Vicar took the Mothers' Meeting." She smiled. "Proper place to quell gossip a Mothers' Meeting is. If you ask me the wind of feeling's changed."

"You mean people are feeling sorry for him?"

"Not so much sorry as feeling that he's had a raw deal, and that they'd like justice to catch up with whoever was responsible."

The words put new heart into Leonie, but before she could fill her wash pan, the landlady pointed to the dresser.

"But as justice takes a little time, it behooves us to do the little we can, so you'll spend the morning designing those posters you once spoke to me about. I've bought paper and paints for you. I'll stick one up in the foyer and one up in the dining room. They'll catch the visitors' eyes there."

Leonie thanked her employer and set to work with a will. By the end of the morning they were finished and pinned onto felt-covered notice boards. Even to Leonie's critical eyes, the curving sweep of the plump fish had a come-hither-and-catch-me look.

"Fair makes you want to reach for the frying pan," remarked Mrs. Laudle, standing back to admire the effect. "Now away you go, and get some roses back into those cheeks again. And tell your brother that from now on, every fish coming into the Duck and Dawdle will be bought."

Acting on an impulse, Leonie turned and hugged her. The situation was unchanged, but one woman's rough kindliness had somehow redeemed the morning. She walked back to Mappins by way of the church, and hearing the staccato clip-clip of shears, looked up to see the Vicar trimming the hedge.

"Good afternoon, Leonie," he called out. "Lend me your eyes a minute and tell me if my alignment is correct. My housekeeper always tells me that my hedge cutting makes her feel seasick."

161

"The hedge does seem to dip a bit here and there."

The Vicar mopped his brow. "I was afraid it did."

Leonie watched him resume his work.

"You do seem to be suffering. Oh, be careful. You're going uphill again." She was silent for a few moments, then said, "If ever I have a garden, I won't have privet. It's so secretive, as if it wants to hide everything from everyone else. Instead, I'll have nothing but flowering shrubs."

The Vicar stopped clipping.

"You love a garden, don't you, my dear?"

"Only since I've come to Mappins. I never used to bother about ours at home. It's so small, so discouraged, and the earth smells of soot and fog. Here it's sweet and crumbly, and it's told me what I want to do when I finally leave school. I shall try to work at Kew Gardens or Wisley."

The Vicar smiled.

"In the meantime, what about your plants for Mappins? When are you going to buy them?"

"I don't think I am ever," she replied, going over the troubling events of the day before. "I . . . I . . . can't prove that I wasn't careless, because you see I could have remembered when it was too late and gone down and rescued the cans and hidden them. I didn't, of course, but I still feel guilty, so I think I ought to send what money I have to Mr. Lester and get him to replace some of the fish. I shan't be able to afford many, but one fish lays an enormous number of eggs."

"It's a praiseworthy thought, but it comes too late," said the Vicar, adjusting his spectacles and squinting through them at the area of hedge already cut. "Dear me! How right you were. I've not only gone uphill, but down as well."

162

"What do you mean?"

"Only that I've bespoken some plants for you. A friend of mine runs a nursery specializing in bedding plants. As it's fairly late in the season, he's prepared to let you have a goodly show at a reduced price. You see, he happened to serve in the Major's regiment and remembers him well."

Leonie's face lit up.

"That's marvelous. And you really think I needn't spend the money on fish? Oh, Vicar! I can't tell you how grateful I am. Do you mind if I go and tell the boys?"

The Vicar shook his head.

"Don't forget to let me know when you want them. I'll run you over to the nursery in the car."

Thanking him, Leonie hurried up the hill and along the edge of the field, where the browning wheat stood almost waist high. Breaking off an ear, she rubbed it between her fingers and ate the sweet, nutty-tasting kernels. As she reached the copse, the sound of voices told her that her brothers were making for the stream. By the time she caught up with them, Ian had already dived from the bank, but Paul was testing the water with a cautious toe, and he grinned sheepishly at his sister.

"It's freezing," he shouted, tossing a ball to his brother. Ian caught it and flung it back so that it landed six inches away from the bank. Paul cringed from the sudden uprush of crystal drops. Now it was Ian's turn to shout.

"You're as bad as Lee. Come on. It's fine once you're wet all over." Paul held his nose between finger and thumb, ran down the bank and jumped. The water near the boathouse was deeper and as it closed over his shoulders his chubby arms ploughed untidy furrows.

163

"Look out for the reeds," said Leonie, who had a particular horror of their underwater treachery.

Her brothers took no notice, but threshed and battled like a couple of playful otters. The fun waxed more boisterous, the ball describing wider and wider arcs, until at length it fell into the center of a thicket of reeds. Instantly a moorhen and a couple of drowsy ducks fled from the spot with flapping wings and indignant cries.

"Leave it to me. I'll get it," said Ian.

Paul trod water as his brother neared the island of green spears.

"See if you can see any nests."

"Look for yourself. The ball's much more important."

Paul obeyed with alacrity. He had read about the clever platform-shaped nest the moorhen built, and now there was a chance he might see one for himself. Holding on to the roots with one hand and parting the reeds with the other, he suddenly gasped with surprise. Nudging the ball with his chin, Ian swam to his side.

"What's up? Found Papa at home or something?"

Paul dragged at the reeds again and there, high and dry in the middle of the floating platform of flattened rushes, were the two missing cans of weed killer.

"Don't touch them," warned Ian. "You don't want to add your fingerprints to those of the wretch who poisoned the fish. We'll get dressed, row here in the boat, use gloves when we pick them up and take them to Sergeant Bowles."

By the time they reached the bank Leonie was so curious she could hardly wait for them to climb out.

"What were you messing about in the reeds for?"

Ian kept his voice low and told her.

164

"So you can stop looking and behaving like the queen of all the martyrs," he went on. "You couldn't throw one can that far, let alone two, and as nothing will persuade you into the water, someone else must have deliberately hidden them there."

"I could have rowed to the island by boat."

"I had the key to the boathouse." Ian took it out of his pocket and wagged it in front of her nose.

"Then they can't be my cans," she argued.

They are, because if you remember, the lids were difficult to pry off," contributed Paul. "Those cans are dented all round the rims."

The relief faded from his sister's face.

"Then if Ian had the key, I *must* have left them on the bank for the mischief maker to pick up. So I'm still guilty."

"Only a tiny bit," said Paul, thinking to comfort her. He screwed his towel around and around as if he were wringing someone's neck. "And just you wait until we find the real villain."

"What hope have you of doing that?"

Paul's look was pitying.

"She doesn't know anything, does she? Fingerprints, of course. We're taking the cans to Sergeant Bowles, and if there are others on them besides yours, then you're innocent."

Mapledon Police Station was housed unpretentiously in an extension built onto the side of a small red brick cottage. In the house itself Sergeant Bowles lived with his thin, red-cheeked wife and three small sons. In the extension, armed only with a telephone, a filing cabinet, a miscellaneous collection of forms and one or two books on law, he kept a watchful and paternal eye on the daily happenings in the village.

The square garden, but briefly glimpsed from the station's one window, was his pride and joy. With its trim borders and neatly bedded rows of geraniums and begonias, it was as orderly as he was himself. Only in the central bed had he allowed imagination full play. Here, in floral letters ten inches high, the blue of lobelia and the white of alyssum spelled out the word POLICE.

Paul stared down at it for some moments lost in admiration; then, obeying the woven instructions on the front mat to WIPE, he followed the others into the station. Sergeant Bowles was busy taking down a statement from Jake.

" 'Tis no excuse, Jake Laudle, and well you know it," he was saying. "Riding a bicycle at night without a rear light is an offense. You'd best spend a little less on cigarettes and a little more on your own and other people's safety. Next time you'll be fined the maximum." He pushed a box forward. "As it is, I'm not booking you this time. Instead,

166

you'll donate a ten-shilling note to the Police Benevolent Fund. And if you don't take that sulky look off your face, I'll make it a pound."

The sight of Jake the bully being forced to eat humble pie was balm to both Leonie and Paul's feelings. Paul grinned openly as Jake tried to make up the amount from shillings and coppers, and when he was sixpence short, made up the deficit from his own pocket. Holding it out, he said, "I'm saving up for my ranch in Canada, but I'll spare you this."

Jake scowled, and knocking the coin from the boy's hand, strode out of the office.

"Ill-mannered pup," growled Sergeant Bowles, retrieving a paper blown down in the wake of the youth's stormy exit. "I'd like to have him under my roof for a few weeks. I'll warrant he'd be a sight better behaved."

"Have you got a cell here?" asked Paul.

"Cell! That's a good one. The only excitement we ever get in Mapledon is a bit of skylarking outside the Duck and Dawdle come harvest time, some youngsters putting silver-paper-covered farthings in the collection plate and a bit of thoughtlessness on the part of lads like Jake."

"What about the Major's trout?" broke in Ian.

"Ah! That were a bit of a puzzle, I admit. But in the absence of any direct evidence, I don't see that I can pursue the matter."

Paul almost danced up and down in his excitement.

"You can, because we've brought it—the evidence, I mean."

Ian took the lid off the box and exposed the cans.

"We've identified them as belonging to Lee," he began, going on to tell the Sergeant how and where they were found.

167

"And we've been careful not to touch them with our bare hands."

"Sensible lads. Looks as though 'tis going to be easier than I thought, because if tests throw up a set of prints other than your sister's, all we have to do is match them."

"That doesn't sound easy to me," said Leonie. "I mean, you can't just go round taking people's fingerprints."

"Everyone knows that, silly," said Paul, giving her a pitying look. "We've got to be squigglier than the serpent."

Sergeant Bowles shook with laughter.

"You're a caution, and no mistake. Squigglier than the serpent. I must remember to tell the wife that." Suddenly he sobered. "Now I'm not saying that anything will come of it. But those two cans spell malice aforethought to me, or to put it plainer, someone with a more than ordinary grudge against the Major. Any idea who that someone might be?"

There was an embarrassed silence. Sergeant Bowles shrugged his shoulders.

"I see you have. Never mind. I won't press you for the name." Paul shuffled his feet restlessly and even the more patient Ian wished that the policeman would get down to tactics. He did in the next sentence. "Now this is my plan of campaign. Leonie works at the Duck and Dawdle. She can keep her eye on Jake, Charlie Sparkes and Mrs. Laudle and bring me something each has handled—an envelope, an empty cigarette packet, anything. Mark each object with the owner's name and hold it by the left-hand corner only. We don't want a confusion of prints. One other thing. Don't bring them to me here. Phone me when the collection is complete and we'll meet at the boathouse. 'Tisn't unusual for me to be seen riding my bike along the towpath."

"What about me?" asked Ian.

168

"You'll look after Gregg. I'll find ways and means to deal with Miss Tracy and the rest of the villagers."

"Miss Tracy!" Leonie was scandalized. "You surely don't suspect her."

"Why not?" Sergeant Bowles locked the box away in his wall safe. "She's not without motive. It can't have been easy to leave the house she loved. Then there was the little matter of being forced to sell Cleopatra's eyes in order to keep the present roof over her head." He shook his head as though in sorrow. "If you knew as much about human nature as I do, nothing would surprise you."

"She does use weed killer," Ian said thoughtfully.

"Ridiculous!" Leonie almost laughed aloud. "She's too old to swim, and she wouldn't have strength enough to throw the cans into midstream. And she couldn't borrow the rowboat because Ian has the only key."

"The Major's isn't the only rowboat. I've got one moored in Crafty Creek. That's the nickname the kids give it because it's so carefully screened by water iris and reeds. I'm not much of a fisherman, but in off-duty times I do a bit of sketching and I like to keep an occasional lookout for poachers. Everyone knows about the boat."

"And you think that Miss Tracy might have borrowed yours, found the cans on the bank, given way to a moment of fury, and then hidden them in the moorhen's nest." Leonie's voice was skeptical.

"I'm not thinking anything beyond the fact that anyone capable of using a pair of oars is not beyond suspicion. Our Miss Tracy may not see sixty-five again, but she's strong or she wouldn't be able to do the amount of gardening she does. So she stays on the list."

169

It was a silent trio who made their way back to Mappins. But in their hearts they knew that Sergeant Bowles had talked sense. Leonie had no scruples about collecting evidence from the Duck and Dawdle, and in the space of a morning she had written names on an empty matchbox, a torn lottery envelope and a whist score card belonging to Mrs. Laudle. Ian and Sergeant Bowles were equally successful, and when two days later the various items were handed over and sent to the neighboring town to be tested, there remained nothing to do but wait.

Bereft of his task of caring for the baby trout, Ian would have found this hard to bear had not Leonie's posters brought results. Soon he was in charge, not only of rods and bait, but also of the packed lunches supplied from the house.

His sister continued to work at the inn, and when in a burst of confidence she told the landlady about her chance of buying flowers at reduced prices, Mrs. Laudle generously increased her wages by ten shillings. Leonie was touched and wished that she could withdraw the score card. Paul, for his part, haunted the police station and on Saturday Sergeant Bowles had news for him. Paul heard it in silence, then, pushing his cowboy hat to the back of his head, he walked slowly and thoughtfully back to Mappins.

In the kitchen Leonie was slicing hard-boiled eggs for the supper salad, Ian was testing a reel and Gregg was oiling the wheels of the outdoor chair. Paul stood in the doorway and broke his news.

"The fingerprints on the weed-killer cans are coming through any day now, and when they do Sergeant Bowles is making an arrest."

170

14 . . . Fight in the Night

"THAT's THE lot," said the Vicar, putting down the last of the potted begonias beside the golden and bronze chrysanthemums. "I confess I'm not sorry. Potted plants are heavier to carry than one imagines." He brushed down the front of his gray alpaca jacket. "I hope you're not disappointed, Leonie, that you didn't after all have the pleasure of making your own selection. But as he wanted space for his prize autumn show, the nurseryman couldn't wait any longer."

Leonie looked down at the closely packed rows of flowering plants standing on the bench.

"Not in the least. They're a wonderful collection. I can never thank you or the nurseryman enough. Will it be all right if I bring you the money tomorrow?"

"Any time will do." The Vicar peered through the half-open door of the boathouse. "I feel quite like a conspirator, but in a very good cause. I wonder if Paul and Ian's inventiveness has run dry yet?"

"Not if I know my brothers," she assured him. "Paul told me that he was going to try to persuade the Major to buy a television set. His favorite cowboy is coming back in a new serial. All for one installment, if you please. We go home at the end of the week."

"So soon! We shall miss you, my dear. I don't know another family who has done so much in so short a time. We shall have to pray for a miracle."

"To keep us here?"

He nodded.

"And don't shake your head, Leonie. If I didn't believe they were still possible, I doubt if I could go on working."

As he said this, Ian came running in, out of breath.

"Have you finished? Good. I stalled Mother and Dad off as long as I could, but now they've decided to have a short walk before supper." He looked at the flowers and pursued his lips in a soundless whistle. "Goodness! It will take hours and hours to plant that batch. Your nurseryman has been jolly generous." He felt in his pocket and drew out five shillings. "It isn't much, but I'd like to make a small contribution. I've ragged Lee enough."

The Vicar took it.

"Yes, he's been more than generous. There must be thirty pounds' worth of plants, but as I've already told you, he was in the Major's regiment. Why don't you get Gregg to lend a hand, or would that spoil the surprise? I'd come myself,

172

but I'm afraid it takes more than an alarm clock to wake me these days."

Assuring him that they would manage, brother and sister waited until they heard his car start up before they locked the boathouse door behind them, and took the shortcut to the kitchen garden.

"I just want to make sure the tools and the watering can are in the shed," said Leonie. "Then we'll have supper and go to bed early. "I'll set my alarm clock for four thirty."

Ian groaned aloud.

"Much too early. You won't be able to see the back of your hand."

"No, it isn't. The sun rises soon after five, and it will take us at least half an hour to carry the plants from the boathouse to the garden."

Ian shook his head.

"How you've changed, Lee. At home we couldn't get you to plan anything. Now nothing shakes you, does it? Not even the possibility that Gregg may be in league with Sparkes or that the Major may be more angry than pleased."

"No, but it will make it doubly hard to leave Mappins." She looked suddenly shy. "Don't laugh, but I want to work with gardens all my life."

"What's so hilarious about that? It's no madder than my decision to become a trout farmer, or Paul's to own a ranch and have lots and lots of horses. He's got all of fifteen shillings saved up towards his passage money to Canada." He pushed open the shed door. The Major's outdoor wheel chair stood against one wall, and above it the rake, hoe and fork hung neatly from brass hooks. Ian pushed aside the chair in the hope of finding the watering can. Instead he saw a large strapped and labeled suitcase. In a moment he had dragged it to the front. "I say! Look what I've found. Gregg's suitcase."

"Nothing strange about that. We all know he's going away for a couple of days."

"Then why take a case this size?" Going to the door, Ian shut and locked it from the inside, then knelt down and began unbuckling the straps.

"Ian, don't."

"Must. If Gregg had nothing to hide he would have left this in the hall or kitchen." Snapping back the locks he lifted the lid. Gregg had not packed tidily, and as socks, pullovers, suits and pajamas spilled out onto the ground, Ian's worst suspicions were confirmed. "So in spite of thinking Paul an idiot for letting on about the fingerprints, he was right," he murmured. "He knew that if Gregg was guilty he would make a break for it. And he is." He sat back on his heels. "There isn't any other explanation for six of everything."

"I still wish you hadn't opened it." Leonie shivered. "I feel just as bad as I did when you opened my journal." She crossed to the window and looked out. Blackbirds and starlings vied with each other in the search for grubs; a thrush banged a snail on a smooth, white stone. All at once these peaceful activities were disturbed by the sudden appearance of Sparkes stepping out from the kitchen. Behind him, Gregg made a threatening gesture. At her cry of surprise, Ian hurried to her side.

"Charlie Sparkes!" he exclaimed. "Now do you believe the evidence of your own eyes? You've got to hand it to Gregg. He's a superb actor."

The two men might be confederates, but there was no

174

love lost between them. With a last glowering look over his shoulder, Sparkes slouched off in a graceless, shambling walk and Gregg slammed the door. Ian restored the case and its contents to its former hiding place.

"Well, that's that," he said, with something akin to a sigh. "In a way it's a relief to know, and I'm glad the matter is out of our hands. Even if Paul's warning has given them time to make plans, they won't get far. Sergeant Bowles is bound to have every escape route watched."

His words only made Leonie feel more miserable. Everything in her resisted the thought that Gregg was guilty. Wrapping the tools in her cardigan she walked silently to the house. Paul met them in the hall.

"I didn't get as far as the television set," he announced. "The Major was going over some accounts with Dad and didn't want to be disturbed. Then Sergeant Bowles arrived, so he was after all."

Ian heard him open-mouthed.

"Then why didn't he make an arrest? He could have nabbed not only Gregg but Sparkes as well."

"He couldn't because he hadn't any evidence."

"N . . . no evidence!" spluttered his brother. "But you said . . . "

"All I said was that the fingerprint results were coming through any day now. But it worked just as it does in a western. Rock Rollston often has to pretend he knows more than he does in order to force the crooks into making a false move. That's what I did."

"You . . . you mean there were no matching sets of prints?"

"No. Whoever used the cans besides Lee wore gloves.

175

That's what Sergeant Bowles came to tell the Major." His gaze fell to the floor. "In a way, I'm glad. I . . . I . . . didn't want Gregg to be arrested. Is . . . is he going to run away?"

Ian nodded.

"We found his suitcase in the garden shed."

A sudden darkening of the hall sent him hurrying to the front porch. Within the space of minutes the summer brightness had been blotted out by the advance guard of storm clouds. Huge and sullen, they brooded over the garden, and even as Paul looked up, the first heavy drops fell. He opened his mouth and let them pound onto his tongue. Leonie pulled him indoors.

"No sense in getting soaked."

"They taste nice, like soda water without the fizz."

The storm was heavy and prolonged, beginning with a few isolated drops of rain and a wind that moaned and slapped at the windows. Then the rain became a deluge, punctuated by brilliant flashes of lightning and the bass rumbling of thunder.

Paul stood at the window counting the flashes, but his sister, who put storms high on the list of things she feared, spared one thought for her parents caught out in it, then ran along the hall toward the small, dark cloakroom. She knew her fear was unreasonable, but each crash of thunder, coming so close upon the revelation about Gregg, seemed to trumpet disaster. As she passed the Major's door, he called out. Leonie hesitated, then went in.

"Oh, it's you, Leonie. The French windows have blown open. I wanted Gregg to close them for me." Leonie pulled them shut, then cowered as another flash illuminated the room. "There's nothing to be afraid of," the Major went on, with unwonted gentleness. "Storms are merely Nature's exclama-

176

tion marks, noisy but necessary punctuations in the midst of summer paragraphs." He patted a seat at his side, then took a carved, wooden box from the low table. "Do you play chess? No? Then this might be the moment to teach you the moves. It will help to take our minds off our problems."

Leonie opened the board and placed it between them.

"Have you so many?"

"Too many to count." He arranged the pieces, named them and explained the moves. Leonie tried to concentrate, but found it difficult to do so. Yet the two games served their purpose, and when at last she looked up, the room was again bright with sunshine.

"Why, the storm's over."

Her companion swept the pieces back into the box.

"We must play again without the excuse we used this time. And I warn you, I shall live up to my reputation and be my normal, ruthless self."

"I . . . I . . . prefer you like this," Leonie answered, "because now I could talk to you—tell you how the library is getting on, for instance." But she got no further.

"Don't make me regret the past hour," he broke in. "What happens beyond Mappins is of no interest to me and never will be."

"You might not always think like that."

"Don't be a fool, child. What encouragement have I to think differently, when my sources of income are systematically threatened? Poachers make a mockery of my fishing rights; tenants whine for improvements, yet when I sanction a scheme that might have proved a gold mine, some villager has to sabotage it."

"Are you sure it was a villager?"

"I'm not sure of anything or anybody any more. Even Gregg talks of leaving me."

"Why?"

"Is the answer so difficult? He's been tried too far."

"Are you absolutely sure that is the reason?"

"Can you think of a better?"

Leonie could but she dared not put it into words. Ob-

serving that the Major was sunk once more in a brooding silence, she tiptoed from the room. On the front porch her mother was shaking the raindrops from her hair.

"What a storm!" she cried. "Luckily for Daddy and me we were within running distance of Miss Tracy's and now I've spoiled my appetite for supper by eating too many of her delicious rock cakes. Were you very frightened, Lee?"

"Yes, but the Major helped. I've been playing chess with him."

"Tell that to the Marines!" scoffed Ian. "You don't know a rook from a pawn."

"Well, I do now, because he taught me."

"Stop arguing, you two," said Paul. "I'm hungry if Mummy isn't."

With the thought of their early rise uppermost in their minds, the youngsters ate an enormous supper and afterwards yawned so loudly that Mrs. Meredith shooed them upstairs.

"Funny how easy it is to pretend you're sleepy when you're not, and how hard it is to squeeze an extra half-hour when you can hardly keep your eyes open," remarked Paul.

"What a sentence," groaned his brother. "I know where I'd put you for English. Right at the bottom of the class." He poked him in the ribs. "What have you got tucked inside your shirt? You seem to be bulging nor' nor' west. Come on, Paul, out with it—and look sharp."

Paul undid his shirt buttons and brought out three apples, three buns and a bag of broken cookies.

"Refueling," he said solemnly. "We're going to be mighty hungry at half past four in the morning."

"Who said anything about you being one of the planting party?"

Paul shot his sister a pleading look.

"You will let me come, won't you? Please. I'm a very good tipper out of pots, and you'll need my rope in order to get your border lines straight."

His brother pushed him toward the bathroom.

"I was only pulling your leg, but mind you're polite when we wake you. Usually it's two hours before we can get a civil word out of you."

While Paul was washing and cleaning his teeth, Leonie wound her small traveling clock. Setting the alarm for four o'clock to be on the safe side, she also got ready for bed. Half an hour later, in spite of their doubts, all three were asleep.

Leonie awoke five minutes before the alarm was due to go off. She was glad, because the bell was shrill and her mother a light sleeper. Pushing back the catch she touched her toes a dozen times to get herself fully awake; then, putting on dressing gown and slippers, she went to wake the boys. Ian roused at her touch, but Paul shrank away and burrowed deeper under the bedclothes. A tug at his hair, and stripping off the bedclothes to his waist, also failed to have any effect, and only when the cold-water treatment was suggested did he open his eyes.

"I felt you first time," he declared, "but I wanted to see how badly you needed me."

"This isn't the time to put anyone to the test," said his sister crossly.

"It is. It's very important to know you're wanted. It makes getting up so much easier—even in the middle of the night."

180

A quarter of an hour later the three met in the kitchen. Leonie lifted a corner of the blue and white checked curtain and peered out. All trace of the storm had vanished, and to the east the overall grayness was thinning as though the invisible fingers of the sun were already at work.

Paul distributed the apples and shared out the cookies and buns, then looped his lariat over his shoulder.

"Quiet, both of you," said Ian. "We'd better eat as we go. Paul crunching an apple is enough to wake the soundest sleeper." He stooped to ease back the bolt on the garden door and found to his surprise that it was undone.

"Why are you surprised?" said Paul. "If Gregg was going, it had to be tonight."

"I simply can't believe it," said Leonie.

"Then you're a silly." Paul's voice was scornful. "I know it's horrid, but with Gregg gone the Major won't be able to part with us. You want to stay on at Mappins, don't you?"

"Only if we're wanted for ourselves." Leonie picked up the trowel and fork. She felt sick and already a little chilled.

Silently they left the house. Silently they crossed the kitchen garden. As they walked, Leonie tried to plan. First they would bring the flowers from the boathouse. Some they would carry and some they would push in the wheelbarrow. Then as soon as there was enough light they would begin planting. Thanks to the storm, digging would be easy. She lifted her face to the still quite stiff breeze and tried not to think of Gregg.

As they neared the boathouse, they heard against the clamor of the rain-swollen stream the sounds of blows, heavy breathing and the scuffling of feet. The youngsters stood motionless, then as curiosity overcame apprehension, they crept forward and parted the curtain of willow fronds. In front of the boathouse, two barely discernible figures swayed and struggled in a close-knit embrace. Leonie touched her elder brother's arm.

"Is . . . is . . . it . . . "

He nodded.

"Yes. It's Gregg and Charlie Sparkes."

15 . . . *Rescue and Revelation*

AT FIRST it seemed that the fight would end in Gregg's favor. His foot movements had a dancing lightness which enabled him to avoid the longer reach of his opponent. Then disaster overtook him. As he swerved to escape an uppercut to his chin he slipped on a muddy patch and fell, striking his head against the boathouse door. Charlie Sparkes seized his opportunity. Without giving his victim a chance to recover his balance he hauled him upright and delivered the final blow. Gregg collapsed and his time did not move.

Ian, who had a ready eye for a skillful fight, even between crooks, found this cowardly assault more than he could stomach. With a cry he sprang forward. Sparkes turned and

braced himself to meet the oncoming rush. The boy's head butted him in the stomach but met a rocklike resistance, and before Ian could get a grip around the man's waist he found himself flung aside as if he were a bale of straw. As he fell, he shouted.

Sparkes hesitated, and then, fearing the sound might have attracted attention, he fended Paul off with one hand and Leonie with the other and took to his heels. Paul ran after him, uncoiling his rope as he did so. Charlie Sparkes was strong, but he had already taken a good deal of punishment, and sooner or later, the boy told himself, Sparkes's step and pace would falter and give him the chance he wanted. What Paul had not bargained for was the sudden appearance of the Major, barring the way in his wheelchair. Calling upon the poacher to stop, he said, "You've done your last bit of thieving, Sparkes, so you may as well give yourself up. You won't get far."

184

Charlie Sparkes, his breath whistling through slack lips, crouched like an animal at bay. Then with a bound that took both the Major and Paul by surprise he leaped behind the chair, turned it with a twist of his strong wrists and sent it careering down the steep bank. In a desperate effort to save himself the Major applied the brake. Somewhere behind him he heard a shout, the pounding of footsteps and the shrill blast of a whistle. Then, as if released from a catapult, he shot head over heels into the dark waters of the rain-swollen stream. He had a momentary feeling of dismay that the water should be so cold, before a stunning blow on the back of his head rendered him unconscious.

Leonie, who had watched the incident in a frozen silence, tried to move. Shock, however, held her rigid. She thought she was shouting for help, but although she mouthed the words, no sound came. Making a supreme effort she dragged herself forward and managed to totter to the spot where the scarred, beaten-down grass betrayed what had happened. She expected to see the movement of an arm and hear the steady, angry voice of the Major telling her to fetch Gregg. Instead, all she heard was the gurgling lap-lap of the racing water, and all she saw was one crazily tilted wheel of the chair.

In a second the full horror of the situation dawned on her. Beneath the half-submerged chair, helpless because of his disability, the Major lay trapped and possibly injured.

"I can't do it," she said to herself, panic stricken. "I'm terrified of water. There will be weeds. They will wrap themselves round my legs like the tentacles of an octopus. I shall be sucked down and drowned." She looked around wildly. Where was Ian, and why didn't Paul come? He had seen the chair plunge. But neither of her brothers was in sight. With

185

one despairing cry she threw herself into the water, and felt its icy clutch rise to chin level.

The shock was almost more than she could bear. But there was no turning back now. Clenching her teeth to stop them chattering she fought her way toward the chair. The bed of the stream was treacherous with slimy green stones. Once she slipped. Water filled her mouth and her nostrils and as she choked and spluttered she felt the first grip of the underwater menace. Once again panic as well as water threatened to overwhelm her. Then, as if a voice had suddenly spoken to her and told her what to do, she ceased struggling and let herself go limp. Instantly the clinging weeds relinquished their hold, and using her hands as paddles, she at last reached her goal.

For a moment she rested to get her breath back, then put her hands to the wheel and tugged. Strength seemed to ebb from her, and when after three attempts it did heel over and fall on its side she almost sobbed for joy. Now her groping hands sought and found the water-soddened tweed jacket. The Major was heavy and she had no knowledge of lifesaving tactics, so she did the only thing possible, holding him so that his head, at least, was above water level. She called again, her voice sounding thin and feeble against the noise of the wind and water, and within minutes, although it seemed longer, there was an answering shout from the bank.

Leonie never recollected clearly what happened when help did reach her. There was a feeling of ease in her aching and numbed wrists, the sensation of strong arms lifting her out of the cold water and the comfort of being wrapped in rough blankets that smelled strongly of camphor. But of the

186

hot drink forced between her blue lips and the ring of faces bent so anxiously over her she had no rememberance at all.

When she awoke some hours later, she found herself in her own bed with a hot-water bottle at her feet and another at her side. She made no effort to move, but lay staring up at the ceiling, letting the events of the early dawn slip into focus. Once again she felt the icy clamor of the water and the unnerving touch of the weeds. But to her astonishment neither had the power to terrorize her any more.

"I'm not frightened," she murmured aloud, "and I never shall be again."

Her mother, who had spent a long and anxious vigil by the window, rose and came toward her. Leonie smiled and removed her mother's hand from her forehead.

"I'm not delirious. I'm feeling fairly all right." She sat up. "How is the Major? Is . . . is . . . he safe?"

Her mother reassured her.

"Thanks to you and some vigorous artificial respiration from Gregg and Sergeant Bowles. He swallowed a lot of water, of course, and he's got a nasty bump on the back of his head where the chair hit him. But Dr. Bailey says that a few days in bed will soon put him right. It was a dreadful shock to all of us." She looked puzzled. "I know this isn't the moment to ask questions, but there's a lot I don't understand, darling. Why were the three of you up at dawn, or Gregg, for that matter? Ian won't tell me and neither will Paul. They simply say it's your secret."

Leonie linked her hands around her knees.

"It still must be, Mummy, but only for a little while longer, I promise."

"Very well. I won't probe." Mrs. Meredith got up. "The boys are simply bursting with pride over what you did. Knowing your hatred of water, I think it must have taken a lot of courage to jump in."

"I very nearly didn't have enough," replied her daughter slowly, "but even though I shall never forget it, I shall never be frightened of water again. That's what I was saying when I woke up. Can I get up?"

"Dr. Bailey would rather you didn't for today, anyway." Mrs. Meredith turned at the door. "But you won't be left out of anything. Gregg's planning a special bedroom celebration tea. Daddy and I are having ours with the Major."

Alone again, Leonie lay and thought how strangely things had worked out for good. She knew what the Vicar would say—that it was a small miracle. Smiling, she dozed again and did not wake until the tinkle of cups and saucers and the squeak of her bedroom door opening roused her.

"I said she would be," announced Paul, taking a flying leap onto her bed.

Ian carried in a folding table onto which Gregg put a loaded tray. Leaving the boys to arrange the crockery, he disappeared, only to return with another, heaped high with biscuits, cakes and sandwiches. Paul was full of the joy of anticipation.

"Isn't it gorgeous? I shall eat and eat and no one will dare stop me because of what I did."

"What did you do?" asked his sister.

"Lassoed Charlie Sparkes. I still can't quite believe it. The rope went spinning over his head first go." Jumping off the bed, he re-enacted the scene. "I was so excited, I pulled the rope too soon and instead of pinioning him by the arms, it tightened round his throat. You should have seen him staggering about and choking. I tried to play him like Dad plays a fish, but mine nearly got away because he whipped out a knife and tried to slash himself free. Luckily, Sergeant Bowles was doing a dawn patrol and arrived in the nick of time. Gee! Was I pleased to see him." It was a long speech for Paul, and at the end he glanced at Gregg and added, "You've got a story to tell us too, haven't you?"

"Not such a brave one as yours and Miss Lee's." Gregg's voice was rough with emotion. "I'm not a fool. I know wot's been going on in your minds. You thought I was up to no good, didn't you?"

For a few seconds his question remained unanswered, then Ian said, "Yes, we did."

"And you were right up to a point. But a chap doesn't have much chance with a cunning twister like Charlie Sparkes for a brother-in-law."

"Brother-in-law!" reiterated Paul.

"That's right." Gregg handed around the filled cups. "It's a long story and goes back to just after the war. Most folks as got through it were lucky. They had 'omes of sorts to go back to. I 'adn't, except for me sister's place. She let me sack out in her sitting room and looked after me as best she could. But somehow I couldn't settle like. Me and her husband, Charlie Sparkes, picked up odd jobs here and there, but nothing reg'lar. Then a bloke wot 'ad a drink with us occasionally put us in the way of earning some easy money. And like a mug I fell for it." His chin sank to his chest as his thoughts drifted back to the past.

"You mean you stole?" Leonie could not prevent herself from sounding shocked.

"As good as," replied Gregg, "though technically I didn't do no more than drive the van with the black-market stuff in it. Then on the fourth run I gets nabbed, see, and by the time I'd done a stretch and got out, my sister was dead." He rapped Paul's hand as he stretched out for the plate of chocolate cookies, and pointed to the plate of sandwiches instead. Then he resumed his story. "You don't know wot it means to 'ave nothing and nobody belonging to you. But I swore I'd go straight, and I did. It was when I was properly down on my uppers that I sees the Major's advertisement. He took me on without so much as a question, and the sight of him so much worse than meself did something to me. At last I'd got someone to care for and work for."

As Gregg's story unfolded and the children learned of his difficulties and his efforts to reawaken the Major's interest in life, their sympathies quickened.

"Go on," said Ian, when Gregg paused for breath.

"Well, out of the blue the Major gets left some money, quite a tidy sum. So he buys Mappins. I thought this was the answer and that he meant to make a go of it. Not on your life. All he wanted was six bedrooms and four downstairs rooms in which to bury himself and his miseries. Six months after we got here, Charlie Sparkes turns up. Don't ask how he knew where to find me. Anyway, he swore he was on the level and asked for a job. After a lot of argy-bargy I persuaded the Major to take him on as odd-job man. I should have known better. Mappins was a soft deal and Charlie didn't intend to lift a finger unless it benefited himself. The one thing he never got tired of was fishing, and when he suggested that there
190

wouldn't be no 'arm in selling some to the villagers and sharing the proceeds, I agreed, Charlie thought I was lining me own nest, when all I wanted was some more money to buy extras for the Major. I should 'ave tumbled to his little game when he got me to make out and sign the bills sent out with the orders. Before long, Charlie was fishing only for his own profit." Gregg refilled his cup, drank thirstily and again resumed his story. "It was about this time that the Major began to get a bit suspicious. For one thing some of the local people started writing to ask if they might fish the stream for themselves as they had done in the past. For another he took to asking me to leave the French windows open at night. I knew wot that meant. The Major was keeping watch. I don't know as 'ow he ever caught Charlie at work, but a week or so later he sacked him for laziness and incompetence. Charlie was furious and swore he'd get even. Worse still, he threatened to show the Major the receipts and put the blame on me, and reveal my past prison sentence."

"Poor Gregg. Would it have mattered so much if he had?" asked Leonie.

"You don't know the Major as well as I do," he replied. "He was always a stickler for honesty in his army days. What's more, he never 'ad no mercy for those that fell by the wayside."

"So you let Sparkes sleep in the boathouse and kept him supplied with food," said Ian. "And you let him go on poaching. No wonder he was wild when we came on the scene."

"With 'im blackmailing me, what else could I do?"

"I still don't understand. How could he get inside the boathouse after I had a padlock put on the door? I carried the key on me."

Gregg again hung his head.

"Not always, you didn't. At first, you hung it on a hook in the kitchen. That's what I'm so ashamed of. I . . . I . . . lent it to Charlie to have a second one cut."

"I see." Ian bit into a cake. "So that's how he managed to get hold of the cans of weed killer."

"And you let the blame fall on Leonie," said Paul. "Oh, Gregg!"

"Do you think I enjoyed 'olding me tongue?" Gregg's voice rose. "I 'aven't slept nights thinking of it. Wot's more, I knew you kids were putting two and two together and getting your sums right. Had been for a long time, too. First there were questions about the torn sleeve, and Miss Lee's sharp eyes noticing the flower caught in the spokes of the wheel."

"You don't mean to say that Sparkes wore the coat and made use of the chair as well as the boat?" said Ian.

Gregg nodded. "They was camouflage, as you might say. He knew no one liked the Major. He also knew that no one, not even Sergeant Bowles, would challenge someone who appeared to be fishing from a wheel chair in his own stretch of water, even though it was late at night. That's how the marks got on the arm. They were dried fish scales."

Ian eased the belt round his khaki shorts.

"What finally decided you to go away for good?"

Gregg looked taken aback.

"How did you know about that?"

Ian told him about the suitcase.

"Don't miss much, do you? Guess you think I'm not much of a crook when I can't even hide me own case properly. Well, if you must know, there were two reasons. I'd had

192

enough of being bullied and blackmailed into silence. And when Paul here lets out about Sergeant Bowlon and the finger prints on the cans, I told Charlie to get out while the going was good. He came up to the house to say he didn't believe me, because he'd worn gloves."

Paul and Ian exchanged glances. "And the second reason?" prompted Ian.

"Was on your account. I wanted to make up for all that Charlie had done, and the only way I could do so was to scram myself. Without me, the Major would 'ave had to take the lot of you on for keeps." His rugged, lined face softened. "He's been a different man since you came. I admit it don't show much as yet, but I can tell."

Gregg's story came to an end at last, but it still left a few questions unanswered.

"If you were already on your way, Gregg, what made you go to the boathouse?" asked Paul.

"A hunch, lad. Charlie was always a mean-minded beggar, and I had a feeling he might do one more mischief. The boathouse seemed to me to be the danger spot, what with the boat he'd repaired and all. And I was right. He *was* there, leaning against the door as cool as you like, smoking a cigarette. I couldn't smell smoke of any other kind, mind, but he had the look of a cat that 'ad been at the cream. Proper festive, he was, too, with his boutonniere the size of my fist. But before I could so much as open me mouth, he stubs out his cigarette and lands me a corker. Why, what's the matter, Miss Lee?"

The flowers!" she said, in an agonized whisper. "The flowers!"

"Flowers! You running a fever?" Gregg appealed to the

boys. "Wot have flowers got to do with me coming a cropper?"

Ian explained and did his best to reassure her, but Leonie would not listen to him. Ignoring all pleas to stay in bed, she tugged on a coat lying across the foot of the bed and thrust her bare feet into shoes.

"I must know," she said. "Jake knew what I was planning for the gardens. Supposing he told Charlie Sparkes. I've got to get to the boathouse."

Treading carefully so as to make as little noise as possible, the three crept down the stairs. After a moment's hesitation Gregg followed. The evening was golden and warm. The wind had dropped to a wayward breeze and the voice of the stream was silent. Nothing remained of the early dawn adventure but the bruising wheel tracks on the grass and the scuffed-up mud outside the boathouse.

Ian unlocked the door, swung it wide and recoiled from the damage revealed. The crushed heads of red and pink begonias mingled with thousands and thousands of white, gold and bronze chrysanthemum petals. In another corner, the battered blooms of dahlias made a colored funeral pyre. Roots and stems lay in twisted heaps among the wreckage of broken earthenware.

Not a plant, not a pot had escaped the systematic vengeance of the wrecker and the sights of such destruction held the onlookers rooted to the spot. Then, with a cry that touched the others to the heart, Leonie fell to her knees and let a trickle of golden petals seep through her fingers.

"He's beaten me, Gregg. I can't try any more," she said in a choked voice.

194

16 . . . *All's Well that Ends Well*

A CHILL, aggravated by the shock of her discovery, kept Leonie in bed for three days. During that time, while her temperature veered between normal and a hundred, she turned an indifferent eye on food and on people. The shattering of her hopes left her inconsolable, but beyond asking her mother to see that the Vicar received the money for the destroyed plants, she did not refer to the garden again.

Paul and Ian, restless now that their stay at Mappins was so nearly at an end, wandered in and out of her bedroom uttering futile words of comfort. Mrs. Laudle sent a chicken and some eggs.

On Friday morning, when Leonie herself knew that

195

she had no further excuse for staying in bed, the Vicar called. Paul showed him up to her bedroom and left them together.

"Good morning, my dear," he began, taking her small hand into his big brown one. "I'm very glad to see you looking so much better. It was a sad, sad business."

"Yes, I'm quite well now."

"Then why aren't you up and out in this beautiful sunshine? Truly, this is a heaven-sent summer. It's made my old limbs feel deceptively young and supple again."

Leonie turned her face to the wall.

"I shall get up tomorrow when we go home."

"So you've turned your back on us already." The Vicar sighed. "I can't say I blame you. You've had a raw deal, but through it you've become something of a heroine to the villagers. And so much can be done in a day." He searched for the right words. "Do you remember what we were talking about when last we met?"

"Miracles!" She could not keep the bitterness out of her voice.

"If you don't like that word, let me use another. You know, the older I get, my dear, the more I find that life works out to a pattern. The material sometimes is poor, the colors smudgy and the threads tangled. Yet the pattern is still there, just as it was the night Charlie Sparkes destroyed the plants you worked so hard to buy."

Leonie winced and again turned her head away.

"I . . . I . . . don't know what you're talking about," she said in a low voice.

"I'm trying to tell you that out of hurt and disappointment something good and durable has blossomed. I've no

196

doubt the clever psychologists of our day would put quite a different interpretation on it, but to me, the good is embodied in one word— charity, or, if you prefer it, love. You'll see the fruits of it if you get dressed and go to the boathouse." He patted her hand. "Don't worry. My little potted sermon is over, and I must take a fresh load of books to Miss Tracy. Friday is always such a busy day at your library, Leonie."

When he had gone she pondered over his words, and thought what a comforting sort of person the Vicar was. The very words "your library" were already making her feel that a small part of herself had been woven into the pattern of village life. Pattern! There it was again. The word teased her. What had the Vicar meant by it, she wondered. How could anything lasting and good rise phoenix-like from the litter of spilled petals and twisted, slashed roots. No miracle could breathe life into them again. All the same she rose and dressed herself.

In the large bedroom shared by her mother and father, Mrs. Meredith was kneeling before a half-packed suitcase.

"Good. I'm glad you're up, darling. How do you feel? A bit wobbly about the knees?" She picked up a handful of socks. "Twelve of them and not a matching pair in the lot. What *does* Paul do with his clothes?" She sat back on her heels, a wistful expression on her face. "How I do hate packing, especially now."

"Don't you want to go home?" Leonie folded one of Ian's shirts.

"Yes, of course, I do."

"You don't sound very certain about it."

"Don't I? I suppose it's because I'm already looking

over my shoulder as it were. A little bit of me will always stay behind at Mappins. Ah well. Mr. Smithers will be glad to see us again."

"You can't do a thing with a cat except let it out and in again," remarked Paul, suddenly appearing in the doorway. "I wish we didn't have to go."

His mother smiled understandingly.

"I know how you feel, Paul. It's hard to pull up roots, even little ones, but as we've no other choice it's no good moping and spoiling our last full day. Memories last a long time. Think how you'll enjoy telling your school pals of the way you lassoed a poacher."

"They won't believe me." He breathed on the brass knob of the old-fashioned bedstead, then polished it with his sleeve. "And I shan't blame them either, because I haven't been able to lasso the post once since then." Hands thrust deep into his pockets, he took his moodiness into the kitchen.

"Poor Paul. He is feeling blue."

"Where's Daddy?"

"Talking to the Major. Did you know that Dr. Bailey says he can sit in the garden tomorrow?"

"And Ian?"

"Digging up bait for the fishermen."

Leonie helped her mother for an hour, then with her own clothes folded, but not packed, she went out into the garden. Against the bright green of the newly springing grass, the flower beds had never looked more empty. Paul joined her as she strolled through the copse.

"Don't you hate last days?" he said. "In fact the last of anything is horrid—last bit of Christmas pudding, last apple off a tree, the last swim—because you know you've got to wait such a long time before it comes round to being the first again."

His sister smiled.

"You do put things oddly, Paul. But I know what you mean."

At the stream, Ian had already filled the last of his cans with bait, and stood wiping his hands on a cloth. Leonie held out her hand and came straight to the point.

"I want the key of the boathouse, please."

"I haven't got it. Gregg borrowed it yesterday evening and hasn't given it back. What on earth do you want to go there for? You'll only be upset all over again."

Leonie repeated what the Vicar had said.

"Curiouser and curiouser," he murmured. "Why did he talk in riddles?"

Paul threw a stone into the stream.

"Because he's a parson, and because he's used to making up sermons. If he didn't give people something to think about, he wouldn't need to preach, would he?"

"You've got something there," agreed his brother, picking a can up in each hand. "Then if you're sure you can face it, let's go. If the door's locked, we can always peep in through the window."

The boathouse was soon reached and the door yielded at the first touch. As it swung open, the three young people stood dumbfounded.

Color was everywhere—on the bench, in the suspended rowboat and along the sides of the walls. In the center, potted marigolds spelled out the word LEONIE.

"Thought you was never coming," said a voice behind them. "Been squinting through that there window until I was nearly cross-eyed." Gregg's face, as he emerged from his hiding place behind the door, belied the abruptness of his greeting. Wreathed in smiles he awaited Leonie's reaction. Speechless for a moment she gazed her fill, then turned and said simply, "Who gave them to me?"

"The villagers. It's their way of redressing a wrong, as you might say, and a last bid to make the Major feel he belongs. What happened sort of woke them up. The library meant a lot and fishing in the stream is attracting visitors. Visitors mean prosperity to the village."

"I'm overwhelmed. I never dreamed of anything like this happening." Leonie walked around and around, looking at a label here and smelling a flower there. "Why, even Jake's given me some plants. Twelve."

"Conscience working overtime, I guess," said Gregg. "To be fair, he's one of the minor miracles the Vicar keeps on about. Seems he was brought up sharp-like when he heard about Charlie Sparkes. Jake's always been a bit of a bully and an idler, but beyond that he's kept his fingers clean. Not like me. Serve me right, if you did tell your pa and the Major." He looked anxiously at them as if fearing they would take him at his word. But on Paul's assurance that they would not, he cheered up again. "By the way, Miss Lee, Jake sent you a message. If you wants any help with the planting, you're to phone his ma at the Duck and Dawdle."

Leonie knew that she would need every bit of help she could muster. That night the alarm clock was again set for four thirty. This time Paul needed no persuading to get up,

200

and was already half dressed by the time his sister came to wake him.

Ian trundled the wheelbarrow, Paul carried a stout tray and Leonie followed behind with two of the largest baskets she could find. Even so, it took far longer than half an hour to transfer the plants from the boathouse to the gardens, and before the first one was planted the shadows were already retreating from the lawn.

Fortunately, the helpers arrived soon afterwards. Gregg yawned his way from the kitchen garden. Jake and the odd-job man who had befriended Leonie on her first morning at the inn came by way of the meadow. The old man pushed the youth forward.

Go on. Say your piece, lad."

Jake responded with a shamefaced grin, muttered a few unintelligible words, then bent to his task of digging holes. By six o'clock, to everyone's astonishment, two more helpers arrived. They were Sergeant Bowles, barely recognizable in cloth cap and pepper-and-salt tweeds, and Miss Tracy, looking most bizarre in three different-colored sweaters and a scarlet woolen scarf worn turban-wise around her head. Protected thus from the perils of dew and wind she kissed Leonie on both cheeks, untied the rubber kneeling mat swinging from her waist and made herself responsible for the borders.

As half-hour succeeded half-hour, the untidy ranks of empty flower pots gave way to a planned tapestry of color. By eight o'clock the last of the labels was tied on and the pots and tools returned to the shed. Gregg went back to the house to brew a much deserved pot of tea and while they waited for it, Leonie drew Miss Tracy back to the terrace to admire the effect from a distance. Her own eyes were alight with the joy of achievement. The old lady leaned heavily upon the girl's arm and at first she had difficulty in speaking.

"It's . . . it's . . . beautiful, my dear," she said at last, "and even if neither of us sees Mappins again, no one can take the memory of this morning away from us. But I'm not going to say goodbye to you, Leonie. You must come and visit me from London." Signaling to Jake to lend her his support, she walked slowly away.

When she had gone, Sergeant Bowles and the children squatted on the terrace balustrade and drank from the steaming cups Gregg handed around.

"How clever of Jake to think of screening off the beds we couldn't fill with those shrubs," remarked Ian. "Promise you won't pull the curtains in the Major's sitting room until we tell you to, Gregg."

"Then you'd best come and lend a hand in the kitchen," Gregg replied. "And if you don't want the Major to start the day badly, see that you don't burn his toast."

Sergeant Bowles went home to don his uniform, and while the breakfast preparations began, Gregg assisted the Major to dress. Three quarters of an hour later Leonie was holding his loaded breakfast tray. As Ian opened the sitting-room door, the adjoining one also opened and the Major wheeled himself in. The surprise of meeting the children so unexpectedly seemed to cause him a momentary embarrassment. Before he could recover, Paul said, "Shut your eyes, Major, and don't open them until we tell you to."

Too astonished to object, he did as he was asked. Ian

swept the curtains aside and flung open the French windows. Leonie put down the tray and with her younger brother's help, steered the chair down the ramp and onto the terrace.

"Now!" commanded Paul.

The Major opened his eyes. The youngsters waited in a breathless silence.

"You . . . you did this," he said, at last.

Paul nodded.

"It was Leonie's idea. She wanted you to have something to remember us by. That's why she took a job at the Duck and Dawdle. It was a horrid job at first, too, because she had to put up with Jake, and Charlie Sparkes."

Bit by bit the story came out and at the end Leonie made her own contribution.

"Then when my plants were destroyed, everyone in the village gave something to make the garden possible. I've put their names down on labels. Come and look."

The Major guided his chair down the path and brought it to a halt between the gay flower beds. The children pointed from one group of flowers to another.

"These are from Mrs. Laudle," said Leonie.

"And those pom-pom dahlias are from the butcher's wife and her four kids," put in Ian. "They emptied their money boxes to buy them."

"And old Miss Tracy gave you the border flowers," piped up Paul, "and Bassett stripped his window boxes of geraniums."

Leonie looked at the Major expectantly.

"They . . . they did it as much for you as for me."

There was no answer. The Major sat with bowed head,

then with a gesture startling in its suddenness, he set the chair in motion and disappeared in the direction of the stream. Paul let out his breath in a sigh.

"He doesn't like them. He's angry."

Ian looked down at his blistered hands.

"I thought I'd got them in a good cause, but I was wrong. You may as well face it, Lee. Nothing will ever change that one hundred seventy pounds of jaundiced outlook."

Breakfast, which should have been a jubilant meal, was eaten almost in silence, and not even their mother's words of praise and pleasure could atone for the Major's silence. To distract them, their father suggested a bus ride into the neighboring town, lunch in a restaurant and a visit to the movie house.

"But we're going home!" expostulated Ian.

"Not until the evening," replied his mother. "The Major has one or two last-minute jobs for me and a few things he wants to talk over with your father."

"Trust him to make sure he gets his pound of flesh," muttered Ian resentfully. "Why don't you both go on strike and refuse? I would." His mother handed him some money and pushed him toward the door.

"Because as Paul would say, we want to do what he wants us to do. Now off you go and enjoy yourselves. But whatever you do, don't miss the four o'clock bus. I shall expect you home to a five o'clock tea."

In spite of their resentment, the young Merediths enjoyed their outing. Though not wisely chosen, the lunch was substantial, and to Paul's immense satisfaction, the main picture proved to be a rip-roaring western starring none other than his beloved Rock Rollston. As battle succeeded battle in the rock strewn canyon, he sat in an unbroken silence. The acrid smell of gunpowder was in his nostrils and the feel of warm horseflesh between his knees. When, after a thrilling pursuit, the villians were rounded up in the full glory of a technicolor sunset, his satisfaction knew no bounds. Ian's voice and repeated nudgings recalled him to his hot seat.

"Look sharp, Paul. Our bus goes in five minutes."

Catching it with only half a minute to spare, the two older Merediths endured a non-stop commentary from Paul which ended only when they stepped into the kitchen at Mappins. To their surprise the house was empty.

"That's odd," remarked Ian. "Mother hasn't even prepared tea. You don't think she could have gone home without us?"

"Perhaps something went wrong at the last minute and we're to be held as hostages," said Paul, only one step removed from the world of celluloid drama. Leonie solved the mystery by opening a note she found propped against the kitchen teapot.

"It's from Mummy. We're to go to the meadow."

Puzzled, they obeyed the summons, then stopped short as they were about to cross the narrow footbridge spanning the stream. The banks on either side were thronged not with visiting anglers, but with those from the village—veterans like Sergeant Bowles and Mr. Dawson the butcher, beginners like Jake.

In the meadow, too, where the hay shocks had been moved to the far end, children dodged about their mother's skirts, their gay cottons looking like spread butterfly wings against the ripening yellow. Away in the distance, looking as if this were a normal, everyday happening, Gregg helped Mrs. Meredith serve tea from a huge, shining urn.

"What does it mean?" asked Ian.

"It's a picnic," said Paul, "and to think Mummy sent us off to the pictures. We might have missed it. Come on."

"She can't have known anything about it," said Leonie.

Paul reached the picnic table first, and at the sight of the plates of buttered scones, buns, sausage rolls and cookies, and the huge iced cake bearing the word *Mappins* in green icing, his eyes nearly popped out of his head.

"Is it someone's birthday?" he asked.

"Mine," answered someone behind him.

Paul swung around and there was the Major, but not the Major of the furrowed brow and surly voice. A large petunia decorated the lapel of his sports jacket and his face had the gentle serenity of someone who had at last come to terms with life.

"Then . . . then you're not angry with me about the flowers after all," said Leonie.

"Angry! You made me ashamed," said the Major. "I was humbled and touched, so touched that I could not trust myself to speak. I owe more than my life to you, Leonie." He was silent, then with something akin to his old brusqueness, he went on: "But what I have to say will keep. In the meantime, do your share of getting rid of this food I ordered from the village a few days ago."

"You mean you planned this, even before you knew about the garden," said Ian.

The Major nodded.

"You're not the only one to have secrets. The Vicar

knew. He supplied the helpers. I only told your mother after lunch, when she had nearly ruined everything by sending you off for the afternoon. Go on, eat."

The children needed no second invitation. The mountains of sausage rolls became molehills; the scones, buns and biscuits began to look as if they had been ravaged by a plague of locusts. The cake was cut with due ceremony and when everyone, including the anglers, had had a piece, the Vicar brought out a hidden pair of scales and the fishing trophy, now polished to a dazzling brightness.

"Fair took be back to the old spit and polish days, that did," said Gregg. "Looks a proper treat now, doesn't it?"

Paul nodded, his eyes sparkling. One by one the catches of the afternoon were weighed. A murmur of delight rippled around the onlookers when Sergeant Bowles's haul tipped the scales at fourteen pounds, but no one was more pleased than he, when in the final totting up of ounces, Jake was found to have beaten him by three.

"Well done, lad," he cried, clapping him on the shoulder. "You take good care of that cup now. I'll be having it off you come the summer of next year."

Jake took his prize from the hands of old Miss Tracy and retreated, clutching the shining emblem of success to his heart. The Vicar stepped forward again and called for three cheers for the Major, but before they could be uttered, the Major raised his hands.

"Cheer if you must, but not for me. It's the Merediths who deserve them. In the space of four short weeks they've shown a love for Mappins and a liking for people I never had."

"But it's catching," said Paul. "You must be beginning

207

to like us, or you wouldn't have given us this scrumptious feast."

The Major smiled.

"Let's say that I'm beginning to be reformed in spite of myself. But don't expect me to change altogether overnight. I'll still be morose and difficult at times. Do you think you can put up with it? Your father seems willing to take the risk, once he has seen a new man installed in his old job."

Ian looked from his parents back to the Major.

"You mean you want us to stay on?"

"He does! He does!" said Paul, turning a somersault for joy.

Leonie said nothing, but stood drinking in the scene before her. The rooks soared black-winged into the blue, sunshine stippled the hay and touched the singing stream with gold, while far away smoke from the train they should have caught drifted across the valley like a skein of white wool.

"Well, Leonie. Haven't you anything to say?" asked the Major.

"Yes." She turned and smiled. "Many happy returns of the day, Major. And there will be, now that we belong to Mappins."